Dark Heart

Dark Heart

By Betsy James
Illustrations by the author

SIMON PULSE
NEW YORK LONDON TORONTO SYDNEY

This book is a work of fiction. Any references to historical events,
real people, or real locales are used fictitiously. Other names,
characters, places, and incidents are the product of the author's
imagination, and any resemblance to actual events or locales
or persons, living or dead, is entirely coincidental.

▲▲▲

SIMON PULSE
An imprint of Simon & Schuster Children's Publishing Division
1230 Avenue of the Americas, New York, NY 10020
Copyright © 1992 by Betsy James
All rights reserved, including the right of
reproduction in whole or in part in any form.
SIMON PULSE and colophon are registered trademarks
of Simon & Schuster, Inc.
Designed by Debra Sfetsios
The text of this book was set in Zapf Calligraphic.
Manufactured in the United States of America
First Simon Pulse edition December 2005
2 4 6 8 10 9 7 5 3 1
The Library of Congress has cataloged the
hardcover edition as follows:
James, Betsy.
Dark heart / by Betsy James.—1st ed.
p. cm.
Summary: Sixteen-year-old Kat's struggle to learn the ways of her
dead mother's people in the hill country is complicated by her
failure in the bear ceremony, a spiritual rite of passage,
and her attraction to the blind outcast Raím.
ISBN 0-525-44951-5 (hc.)
[1. Fantasy.] I. Title.
PZ7.J15357Dar 1992
[Fic]—dc20
91-45319
CIP
AC
ISBN-13: 978-0-689-85070-7 (pbk.)
ISBN-10: 0-689-85070-0 (pbk.)

~ For Jeanne ~

YOUNG WOMEN'S SONG

Look at me. You can't have me.

> Please let's dance!

Come to me. Don't touch me.

> Please let's dance!

Tell me your name. I'm not listening.

> Please let's dance!

Under the moon,

Long before the morning,

As if I loved you,

> Please let's dance!

YOUNG MEN'S SONG

We came because they needed us.

> Hey!

It looked good to us, so we came.

> Hey!

We'll go back when we want to.

> Hey!

But if the food's good,

The girls good,

The music good—

Maybe we'll stay!

> Hey!

NOISY AS STARLINGS, the unmarried girls of Creek poured out of the north gate, their empty water jars on their heads. By the forbidden, smoky lodges of the Loom Holds they surged back laughing, because the young men blocked the way.

They always blocked the way. The young men sang,

> Waiting at the den.
> Maybe the bear comes.
> Oh, yes!

Waiting in the winter.
Maybe the spring comes.
Oh, yes!

Kat staggered in the jostling crowd. The young men never bothered to tease her, because although she was sixteen she was not a woman yet. She rescued her wobbling jar and held it in both arms.

All the girls except Kat wore embroidered dancing skirts, and even on this frosty late-winter morning their blouses were cut low to show the blue tattoos on their breasts. Kat wore childish culottes, and a pinafore. The young men strutted like peacocks in their kilts and greatcloaks, short cudgels shoved into their sashes.

Tossing their spindles, the men locked shoulders and laughed. One of them yelled, "What will you give us to let you through?"

"Cold rabbit pie that the dog won't eat!" shouted Jekka, Kat's cousin.

"We'll warm it." That was handsome Set, the headwoman's grandson. His cloak and coxcomb hair were scarlet, his long legs insolently bare. "Hey, darlings, we'll warm *you*!"

The girls shouted back, "Naked rooster!" "Set, where are your stockings?"

"Jekka jaybird, who'll kiss such a big beak?"

"Watch out, rooster! With my beak I'll steal your spindle!"

Laughing, Set drew from his fist a length of carded wool, flicked his spindle down, wound up the new coarse yarn, and answered, "Don't bother, jaybird. I want a sweeter girl."

"Set has a honey!" The young men whistled and stamped. "Who is it? Show us, Set!"

Set strolled in front of the girls.

They jeered.

He looked them over, and stopped in front of Kat.

"She's a little red cub," he said. "Not grown yet, a first-moon bear's child."

Kat stared at him blankly.

Jekka leaned over and hissed, "Answer him, Kat!"

"What?"

"It's you. He's courting you. Answer him quick!"

The young men catcalled. "Set loves a cub! A cub!"

Kat clutched her jar. Shame swelled into her arms and face until she was as red as her curls and could not feel her hands.

"Tell him, 'This cub has claws!'" whispered Jekka. "Shout this: 'This cub *eats* naked rats!'"

But Kat stood dumb, as though the frost had frozen her. With a crow of laughter, Set tossed his spindle into her water jar.

The men roared.

Kat snatched the spindle out and threw it on the sand. "Stop it!" she said, like a child.

Plump Mía took pity on her, shouting to Set, "Come throw your spindle in *my* pot. I'll test your yarn!"

"I'm not stupid." Set grinned. Mía was as tall as he was. He picked up the spindle and tapped it clean against his long thigh. The wall of shoulders opened and the girls ran through, laughing and shouting insults, past the Loom Holds and onto the wide plain of the mountain valley.

"You'll have to be quicker," Jekka said cheerfully to Kat. "Set has a wicked tongue. But his legs are nice."

Still crimson, Kat said, "Why did he do that? Nobody ever—"

Esangi cut in. "Don't think it means he likes you. They always bait the girl who's going to her bear.

You'll have to learn to fight back if you want to be a woman."

"Oh," said Kat in a small voice. Struggling to balance her jar, she followed the girls down the path to fetch water from the sacred spring. The water was for her, because she was going to be eaten by the bear.

2

KAT TROTTED to catch up with her cousin. "Jekka," she said in an undertone, "does it hurt?"

"What?"

"The bear."

"The tattooing's the worst. It's like hornets, and it goes on and on." Jekka looked down at the necklace of inky spirals on her own breasts. "You've got less to tattoo. Lucky."

"No, I mean, does it hurt—"

"When she eats you?"

Selem and little Bo had been eavesdropping. Bo

piped up, "It's your spirit she eats, cub. Your girl-hood." She and Selem were only fourteen, but they were women already.

Selem laughed. "You're ignorant and sweet like a baby, Lisei."

"I'm not Lisei," Kat said coldly. "Lisei was my mother."

"Everybody says you look just like her. Why did your mother run off with that Leagueman?" said Selem.

"She loved him."

"Leaguemen are bad. Maybe other villages like those traveling merchants, but we don't let them come to Creek anymore. Your mother must have been crazy or cursed, to run off and get you born in that foreign place. When you first came to Creek you didn't even talk right."

"Shut up, piglets," said Jekka. "Things were different when Kat's mother was a girl. The Leaguemen came to Creek all the time. They unpacked their mules in the square."

"Leaguemen rape women," Esangi said from behind them.

Esangi was the best potter among the unmarried girls. She was not tall, but she was wiry and strong from working the clay. She had a hard fist and she used it; and she hated Kat. Kat did not know why. It was one of the thousand bits of common knowledge that had gone over her head during those first months in Creek while she struggled to learn the language. Now she was afraid to ask about it.

Esangi said, "Leaguemen are wild dogs. That's why we kicked them out of Creek."

"Nobody wanted your opinion," Jekka muttered. She turned to Kat and said, "Listen, cousin, about the bear. When a woman dies, we bury her beside her threshold with her grinding stone, and over her body we plant a rose. That's why there are so many roses in Creek. But her spirit goes to the wilderness and enters a bear."

"I know that already."

"Then act as if you do, or those squeakers will tease you. The hunters catch the bear. The bear eats *you*, and you become the bear. Her spirit takes you up the mountain—up Dark Heart—and teaches you. Then you're a woman, safe in the Circle." Jekka looked thoughtfully at Kat. "Your mother's dead. Maybe it's *her* spirit that's in the bear the hunters brought. How strange—you'd be eaten by your own mother."

Kat thought of the bear she had not yet seen, which groaned and thudded in the thick-walled pen behind the Bear House. She shivered, saying, "My mother died far away!"

"What difference would that make to a ghost?"

"The *only* way to get to be a woman is to be eaten by the bear?"

"Yes. Well, now, anyway. It was different in the old days, when everybody lived in the Tells."

As Jekka spoke she glanced to her left, then glanced away. The line of girls was passing the Tells: the ruins of a town much larger than Creek that sprawled along the path for a mile or more. Nothing was left there but stones heaped in scabby hummocks. The Tells were full of evil spirits.

Jekka said, "In the old days the hunters didn't bring a girl her bear. She went up the mountain by herself, looking for it. But imagine, cousin: if a girl were just to walk into the wilderness with her soul open, asking to be eaten—what might get her?"

"*Anything,*" said Bo, who had sneaked up on them again. "Maybe the bear—but more likely a ghost or a demon."

"Or a piglet," said Jekka, glaring. "Do you mind?"

"Kat's a cub," said Bo. "We women get to teach

her things. Cub, the people who lived in the Tells were cursed. They went up the mountain alone and got eaten by devils. Ouma cursed them, and all but one of their springs dried up. Everybody died except the good people, and *they* built Creek."

On the red, rotten mounds of stone a hawk clung to a ruined archway and screamed.

"Well, now we know better," said Jekka. "We make sure it's the bear that eats you. You'll see, cousin—it'll be fine." She smiled at Kat. "You can choose a man then too. But watch out! That Set will be at you like a hound puppy. Sharpen your tongue, cousin, or he'll kiss you quiet!"

"He was making fun of me," said Kat, but so softly that no one heard. She looked around, covertly, at the other girls.

Like her, many of them had red or reddish curls. But Creek girls wore long braids coiled around their heads like crowns, while Kat's hair was a short, horrible mop that flopped into her eyes.

Initiated Creek girls wore embroidered skirts and petticoats, ribbons and perfume from the shop in Ten Orchards. Their blouses showed off their breasts. Kat wore a child's culottes and the pinafore that had been Jekka's before she went to her bear.

She was slight and small; the babyish hand-me-downs fit her too well.

Creek girls were clever. When the boys baited them in the streets they gave as good as they got. But when the young men came strutting in their brilliant cloaks Kat went blank completely and could only scowl.

Full of shame, she thought of the expectations she had had on the day she first came to Creek.

That had been winter, more than a year ago. For nine days she had jolted inland on the high seat of her aunt's mule cart, through winding valleys and friendly low hills. Then from the eastern curve of the earth, mountains had begun to rise—like ghosts, then like castles, then like gods.

Among them one was tallest. Even in the sunlight it had seemed to be in shadow, its dim peaks streaked with snow.

"See her raise her head!" Kat's aunt Bian had said, pointing with the cart whip. "That's Dark Heart, Ouma's mountain. She stands above Creek. When I see Dark Heart I know I'm almost home."

Kat had been awed and afraid. She had never seen a mountain before. She had lived her whole life by the sea, and she was in love with a man there—Nall, who belonged so completely to the water that he thought of himself as a seal.

But this new world was all stone and sky. It was bare and spare and high, ringed by mountains. The only water came from the snow, the sudden rains, and the braided creek that had given the town its name.

With her eyes on Dark Heart, Kat had whispered, "I thought my mother came from a *Hill* town."

"So she did, my cub," Bian said, smiling. "Creek lies in the valley, along the gentle foothills. Do you think Ouma the Bear Mother wants us meddling on her mountain? Our men go into the wilderness to hunt, but Dark Heart they leave alone."

"Why is it—I mean, why is *she* called Dark Heart?"

"Because that has always been her name."

The mule cart had bumped along the frozen track until Kat could see the foothills, brown and rolling, and then the town of Creek itself, its ranks of poplars and its crooked walls, its warm stone houses with red tile roofs brambled over by the gray lace of winter rosebushes.

People came running, shouting. Terrified, Kat could not understand a word. Her father had never allowed his wife to speak her own language.

But Kat thought, I'll learn to speak. I'll learn everything. I've run away from Father, and now Mother's people will teach me who I am. Besides, I'm a woman already. Nall kissed me.

She gathered her courage and slid down from the high seat, into the hubbub that was Creek.

But after a year among the girls of Creek, Kat realized that she was so childish, funny-looking, and ignorant that Nall must have kissed her out of pity. Yet the bear would save her. As she hopped to keep up with the others on the creek path she thought, In three days the bear will eat me and I'll *really* be a woman—beautiful and worthy and wise. Then I'll go back to Nall, and he'll love me.

The track dropped down among the wild olives and crossed the stream on stepping-stones. Blue rags of snow shone in the shadows. Scrambling up the far bank, the girls crunched over dry grass to the foothills, through the juniper wood to the steeper slope. There, in the silence of Dark Heart, even Selem and Bo stopped whispering.

As the first sun lit the treetops they came into the clearing, hearing the chuckle of the spring.

Among a scrub of willow the Blessing Tree, a huge cottonwood, grew out of the hillside and straddled the pool. Prayer ribbons fluttered from its lowest branches.

"Look—some weaver's left an offering," said Jekka. "Black cloth."

But the heap of cloth rose up.

It turned into a young man in a black cloak, with bare legs and scarlet hair. His handsome face was rigid with rage.

"The devil!" he said contemptuously. "I'd forgotten today was the hens' pilgrimage."

"It's Set!" said Kat.

The man at the tree laughed, an ugly sound. "Look again, my chickens."

It was Set's older brother, Raím.

He did not live in town. Kat had rarely seen him. He had Set's densely freckled face and long body, his arrogant back; but his eyes, which should have been merry and teasing, were like blue glass in his face.

Raím was blind.

He rubbed his eyes. They were wet, for he had been bathing them in the spring. "Sorry I'm not the cock of the hen yard, darlings," he said. "I know you're disappointed."

14

Jekka made a rude hand gesture at his unseeing face, but her voice was formal and sweet. "Mother's peace be with you, Raím."

"Jekka." He identified her instantly.

"We'll wait until you're finished."

"Oh, I'm finished. I was finished long ago." He stooped and felt for his aspen staff. Then he paused, and asked, "Where's the bear bait?"

Pitying his blindness, Kat squeaked, "Here I am."

"I've forgotten your name."

"It's Kat."

"Ah! The Leagueman's kid."

Her compassion curdled to dislike.

"Speak your name again," said Raím.

She threw it at him. "Kat!"

"Now I've got you." Half his mouth flinched into a grin. "I collect birdcalls. Little sparrow voice, take care what the bear eats."

He turned abruptly and went on up the path, knocking on the rocks with his staff.

Kat said, "What a nasty man!"

Jekka shrugged. "Don't mind. Raím's always sarcastic, the way Set is always teasing. They're both obnoxious."

"You were stupid enough to tell him your name,"

Esangi said. "If you want to be a woman you'll have to learn to keep the upper hand."

The Blessing Tree was of enormous girth. Its branches, living and dead, were still bare of leaves, but they were bright with generations of offerings to Ouma the Bear Mother: clay rattles, spindle whorls, goat bells, rain-withered baby shoes. Lightning had dug a hole in the first fork of the branches, and there a sleeping beehive spread its wattles, brilliant yellow.

The tree's huge roots made a cavern over the pool. Or perhaps the spring had carved the earth from beneath the roots, for from far back in that darkness came the chime of water.

This was the one spring that had not dried up because of the sins of the Tells. Now it was used only for ceremonies—like the water-gathering for a bear fast.

Kat swung her water jar from her head and looked at it. She had made it herself. It was lopsided, but she had painted it painstakingly with the Bear's Eye sign. Jekka was singing,

> Out of the first place,
> Little river,

Blood beginning,
Over and over.

Out of the dark place,
O our mother!
Grief and children,
Over and over.

Jekka stepped to the round slab in the middle of
the pool, steadied herself by gripping a root that was
worn with touching, and dragged her jar through the
water. She leaped to the far bank and stood poised
like a jay on a twig, the dripping jar on her hip.

"Now Mía," she said.

"*Out of the first place,*" Mía sang, sweeping the
pool with her jar. Esangi, Sara, Ruma, and Kos followed, then Elanne and Bárteme, Arra, Gaími, Gel,
Selem, and little Bo, who hopped to the far bank
like a chickadee and piped, "Now Kat!"

The song was easy. "*O our mother,*" Kat sang.

Then the familiar strangeness came down over
her body. It was as though she stood outside the
world as well as in it, confounded by it, so that
what was thoughtless and natural for Jekka and Bo
was baffling for Kat. She wobbled on the round

17

slab, missed her grip on the root, and had to save herself by snatching at a purple ribbon; she nearly dropped her jar, which was slippery as a newt, and when she leaped she landed short. She slithered back into the winter watercress and sat down in the pool with a splash.

"Cousin!" said Jekka.

Kat waited for Ouma the Bear Mother to strike her dead.

Nothing happened. A jay cackled scornfully from a juniper bough.

"Come out of the water, ninny."

The fondness in Jekka's voice made no difference. Bo was tittering behind her hand, and Esangi looked bored and triumphant. Kat sloshed to the bank. Jekka put down her hand and hauled Kat up—neatly, the way Jekka did everything.

"We'll do it again," she said. "The Mother knows you're a Leagueman's child."

"You have to do everything perfectly, cub," said Esangi. "If you want to be a woman."

"You should pray to Ouma," Mía said. "She'll help you if you hang an offering on the tree—something dear to you."

18

"I don't have anything," Kat said, her teeth chattering.

But as she said it she thought, with a chill that was not from cold, that she *did* have something—something very dear.

"You'll freeze," Jekka was saying. "Take off your culottes and I'll loan you a kirtle. Who's small who can loan a petticoat?" She was stepping out of her plainest overskirt, the one with no embroidery.

"She can have one of mine," said Selem. "As long as we don't meet the men on the way back—I'd feel half-naked!"

Kat fumbled out of her wet culottes. She picked them up in a heap, put the dry clothes over her shoulder, and with her legs scarlet from cold walked up and around to the mountain side of the Blessing Tree.

"Where are you off to?" said Jekka.

"To pray for a minute. They said to."

"In your bare bottom?" But after one curious stare the girls courteously turned their backs.

Behind the tree's broad trunk Kat groped in her sodden pocket. She drew out of it a piece of carved ivory and laid it along her finger.

It was a little seal, the length of her thumb

joint. Its flippers were sleeked along its sides and its head was raised as though it listened. It had whiskers, and a clear stare like a cat's.

Kat thought of Nall, who had made it for her. She thought of the warmth of his mouth.

She looked at the tree. One lobe of the beehive was just within reach. A few cold bees trembled in the winter sun.

Kat closed her eyes.

"Ouma, Mother, eat my childhood. Make me beautiful and normal. Make me a woman—for him, Mother. For him."

She kissed the seal. Then, as high as she could reach on tiptoe, she pushed it under the edge of the beehive, next to the wood. The sleepy bees brushed her knuckles; her fingers came away smelling faintly of honey and summer.

She put on Selem's petticoat and Jekka's over-skirt and squelched back around the tree in her wet clogs.

"I'm ready now," she said.

They did the water ceremony again, with Kat last. And it was as though an outer hand sustained her—as though in burying the little seal she had buried all the darkness that confounded her and made her stumble. Light as a lark she leaped from stone to stone, over the surface of the water.

Even Esangi said grudgingly, "That might do."

"Your hair's too short to braid," said Jekka as the girls walked back along the creek to the fasting hut, "but I'll brush it till it shines. Tomorrow morning you'll enter the hut with the water the Mother has given you. Three days—then you'll go to your bear."

A jaunty whistle rang from the willows.

"It's the men!" yelped Selem.

But it was Set, alone, raising his head like a stag and grinning at Kat as she walked with her shining jar. He sang,

> Waiting by the path.
> Maybe my love comes.
> Oh, yes!

He blew her a kiss.

3

THE CRACK UNDER the door grew pale with dawn.

Kat had watched it brighten and dim three times. Alone in the little cubicle, she watched the rod of sunlight that slanted down through the smoke hole travel three times across the sandy floor and fade against the wall.

She had to tend the fire day and night, or freeze. She wore nothing but a white cotton fasting skirt. Beside her, full of water, was her clumsy jar; when it was empty, old deaf Kiku shuffled in and filled it again, bringing more firewood without a word.

Once each day the women came, immense in bearskins, to teach Kat the songs. She knew Jekka and Bian were among them, but she could not recognize them. Their clay masks were identical black bear faces, with red muzzles.

By the second day even their voices sounded strange. Kat repeated the songs and was left alone. She raked the floor smooth of footprints and knelt again, hugging her arms around her body.

She tried not to think of the bear that moaned and snuffled in the pen behind the Bear House. Instead she made up a chant, *"Please don't hurt me,"* and sang it mixed with the bear songs.

> Foot like my foot, Mother.
> (Please don't hurt me!)
> Hand like my hand, Mother.
> (Please let it be over!)

Old Kiku snored outside the door.

Kat dozed. The light grew brighter. In a dream she stood by the sea and called to the seals on the beach—but they left her and dove into the water. The last one looked back over his shoulder. He had a human face.

"Nall!" she screamed.

"Wild dogs howling," muttered Kiku.

Kat put her hands to her mouth. Who had screamed? Outside she heard a shuffle and the click of claws. The door swung open, letting in the mountain wind.

They had come to take her to her bear.

Kiku ducked in under the lintel. "Get up, Lisei," she said. "It is your time."

Kat said stupidly, "I'm not Lisei." As she rose the door frame tilted.

"Slowly, child."

She held on to the doorpost. The bodies of women in bearskins blocked the light. The whole world smelled like bear.

They put a black wool blanket over her shoulders. "Come, daughter," they whispered, and she went with them, barefoot on the frost.

Dark Heart was dim with morning mist. On stepping-stones the procession crossed the creek with its crackling skirt of ice, climbed the bank, and came through the south gate into the Clay Court, which was forbidden to men as the Loom Holds were forbidden to women. The potting sheds were smoked with frost. The women passed the red inner gate into Creek itself and walked the colonnaded streets to the central square.

There was a big fire on the Hearthstone. People stood in silent groups. No uninitiated children were there—but there were men. Kat had not known there would be men.

They were the hunters who had brought her bear, dressed in the vivid cloaks they wove for themselves in the secrecy of the Loom Holds. Kat's uncle stood among them. He would not look at her. The sun came over the shank of Dark Heart and kindled her fiery hair.

"People of Creek!" cried Wenta the headwoman from behind her mask. "Say good-bye to your child."

"Good-bye," murmured the villagers.

Set came strolling, late as usual. "Good-bye," he drawled, and yawned.

The women led Kat across the trampled sand to the Bear House. The bear pen was silent. The bear was not there.

At the stone portal of the house, someone—Kat thought it was Bian—pulled the blanket forward over Kat's face. She was grateful. She did not want to see.

They led her into the Bear House.

Gazing down under the blanket, she caught

glimpses of shadows, firelight, feet. She heard something snuffling.

The bear chant began.

> Foot like my foot, Mother.
> Hand like my hand.
> Back like my back, Mother.
> You stoop, you stand.

Low and coaxing, the headwoman's voice said, "Ouma! Eat this child. Take her up the mountain and teach her in the dark. Send her back to us a woman."

The snuffling grew louder, and it became a hoarse, high squall. Was it in front of Kat? Behind? Her body tried to crowd back away from the blanket.

"Bear, house of our dead," the headwoman crooned. "Who are you? In your body, whose spirit has returned to teach us womanhood?"

The hair rose on Kat's neck.

It *is* my mother's ghost, she thought. It's Lisei.

Dizzy with fasting and terror, she panted under the heavy, sheep-stinking blanket, and in that instant the blanket was pulled away.

She stood alone in the middle of the Bear House, naked to the waist. Straight ahead of her Set lounged among the hunters, with a look in his eyes that was both scornful and afraid.

She was hot. She was cold, and white as bone. Everywhere were men's eyes; her darting, terrified glances searched the crowd for cover, but everywhere she was exposed.

Except to one man. In the shadow of an archway, scowling, stood Raím.

He could not see her. With a sob Kat fixed her eyes on his blind ones. She straightened her back.

"Spirit without place," said the headwoman. When Kat did not answer she repeated it. "Spirit without place!"

"I am . . ." Kat gasped, groping to remember the ceremony. "I am that spirit."

"You were a child. Now you are only spirit. Come, be eaten by your destiny, and be a woman." From the bearskin the headwoman held out her big-knuckled hand. "Come, Lisei."

In the silence Kat heard herself say loudly, "I'm not Lisei! I'm not my mother! I'm Kat!"

"What does it matter who you are, girl? Come to your bear, and be made a woman as your mother was!"

Slowly Kat raised her hand. Her wrist was gripped in bony fingers and she was turned around, stumbling. When she righted herself, there in front of her was her bear.

It was puny.

It was a young red female, swinging her weight from foot to foot. She strained against the cord that tethered her to a post, her fur pressed crooked by the harness. As Kat stared she lunged with a snarl, snubbing herself on the rope.

"Sing to her," said the headwoman.

Kat opened her mouth. No sound came out.

"The bear chant," said the woman. "Sing!"

"*Foot like my foot, Mother,*" Kat began.

But other words rushed to her mind: *Please don't hurt me!*

"*Hand like my hand. Back like my back, Mother. . . .*"

There she stuck.

The headwoman made a little scolding sound. "Kneel down."

Kat knelt.

"Sing to your bear. Look into her eyes, let her know you. Draw closer. Enter her cave; stroke her fur; kiss her, your bear." The headwoman's voice was a whisper. "Go to your bear!"

Kat leaned forward. She looked into the bear's eyes.

"*Foot like my foot,*" she began, and stopped.

"Sing!"

"*Hand like . . . Hand like . . .*"

The bear's face grew darker, grew huge. The bear's eyes, seeing her, were a cave; they pulled her down, pulled her in, unmaking her, making her into a bear—into her mother, all mothers, faceless in common womanhood.

Behind her the cave door shut.

"*No!*"

She tore her eyes away, thrust her hands at the bear's face and screamed, "*I don't want to be eaten!*"

The bear's forearm flashed like a boxer's. Claws raked Kat's breasts. The floor became the ceiling, there was a snarling bark, shouting, the sound of running feet. She rolled away and for an instant stood, seeing the eyes of the whole village horrified—all but Raím's, which were motionless, blue and puzzled, for he had seen nothing at all.

Then she fell.

4

"THEY AREN'T HEALING," said Bian.

Kat sat on the edge of the bed, her legs dangling like a four-year-old's. Through the half-open door she could see the day's-end fire and the bustle around the hearth. Jekka washed off mud from the potting shed, and her small brother, Mamik, tossed his spindle. Emmot sat weaving at the common hearth loom that women could look on. As the now-familiar ritual in the bedroom went on, all of them kept their eyes carefully away from the door.

"By now they should have healed," said Bian.

Her warm, open face was tired and strained. These days it wore no other look. Almost three weeks had passed since the bear ceremony, and the dressings on Kat's chest still came away stained and damp. The wounds were not angry anymore; they oozed, they were pale and dull as Kat was pale and dull. They refused to close, and since the bear Kat had refused to go outside.

"Little cub," said Bian at last, pinning the fresh bandages with a brass pin and lifting Kat's face, "put on your clothes. Go walk, just once. Let the sight of the hills heal you."

"I won't go out. I won't wear culottes, or that pinafore. I'm not a child!"

"Lisei, you must."

"I'm Kat!"

"Kat." The lines of Bian's forehead deepened. "You know the Circle would have sent you away. What nonsense, to think you'd bring a curse on the babies! But people are afraid—in the memory of the grandmothers, no girl has failed her bear.

"I've fought for you, bargained. It was not your fault. You're a Leagueman's child! I didn't teach you well enough. You're *my* daughter now, and I say there's no curse."

With hands that had buried four of her own children, Bian stroked back Kat's mop of hair. "You must have another bear. But till then you are still a cub, and you must wear a cub's clothing." She took up the threadbare blouse. "We'll dress you warmly, and you can look at the sun before he goes. Come home to supper when you like, and Jekka will practice the bear songs with you before you go to sleep."

Kat slid off the bed. It was not worth fighting about. Nothing was. The dull burn of the wounds was welcome; it made tangible other, less visible misery. She took the blouse and jerked it over her head roughly, to make sure it hurt.

"I don't need help dressing," she said. "I'm fine."

To prove it she tied the green sash that Emmot had woven for her.

"Don't forget, you must drink this," said Bian, holding out a mug of stinking healer's tea.

Kat took the handle in her left hand, watching the steam waver upward. Her hand looked so far away, as though it were leaving her—like any chance at loveliness or love, like the seals in her dream. Like Nall.

She could think of no reason to hold on to the

mug. Hypnotized, she watched as her distant hand let go.

The mug fell in slow motion, drawing through the air a glassy arc of tea, and smashed on the flagstone floor.

"Cub!" cried Bian.

Jekka came running, with Mamik crowding after her, hiding in her skirts.

"My hand let go," said Kat, staring. "I'm not strong again yet."

But she knew that was not why she had dropped the mug. And she knew that Bian knew. Terrified, she gabbled, "I should go walk. I'll walk. The air will be good. Bian, I'm sorry!"

"It's nothing, nothing, an old cup."

"I'll sweep," said Jekka.

Mamik said, "Mama, if it was me you'd be mad."

Jekka came back with the broom and spanked him with it, saying, "Don't be a pig to your mother!" She was crying. To Kat she said, "You go take a walk. Don't mind what anybody says. If they bother you, you tell me." She rolled up her sleeves and began to brush the wet shards into a heap.

A purple bruise glowed on her elbow. She pointed to it. "See? Esangi did that. But I punched her mouth first. If she says again that you'll bring a curse on the village, it'll be through a fat lip."

"Take care, cub," said Emmot from the hearth.

"Thank you," said Kat. Looking at their worried faces, she added hopelessly, "You're kind," and left the house. With the tail of her eye she saw Bian sit down on the bed and weep.

The sky was a purple roof of cloud that hid the mountain heads. In a few windows early lamps were lit. Children straggled home from the mill with buckets of ground corn; when they saw Kat they whispered and scrambled around corners and down alleys, until Kat was walking in an empty street.

She turned east toward the creek. She would go watch the mill wheel in its numb round. A woman with a baby on her arm stepped out of a blue door; seeing Kat, she snatched her shawl across the baby's face and banged the door shut.

Kat turned another corner. Curtains were quietly drawn, and toddlers playing on stoops were pulled indoors.

She fled down the street. At the east gate she looked back; people were putting their heads around the doors, peering after her. At her glance all the heads popped out of sight again, like prairie dogs down burrows.

She ran out the gate, north along the creek path. Above the town walls the naked poplars made a whipping sound.

Beyond the town she slowed to a fast walk. She realized she was on the path to the Blessing Tree. Blindly she turned off onto the plain, where a net of tracks ran among the greasewood and faded thistles.

The musky, male tang of burning cedar warned her away from the Loom Holds. She caught a glimpse of carved beams, of a dead doe racked on poles where the town dogs skulked. All the cedar doors were shut. She turned north again and walked on heedlessly, following path into path until all paths ran out.

Under her feet were scattered potsherds—hundreds, thousands. Hillocky land rose up rough and full of stones, with here and there a heap of fresh dirt scratched from a badger's hole. Animal tracks were everywhere, crisscrossing the sand. She had come to the edge of the Tells.

She turned back toward Creek.

Hardly a bow shot away, Set sauntered cross-country, in one hand his hurling cudgel and in the other a dead pheasant, open-winged.

Kat crouched down behind a clump of sage.

He was beating the grass for quail. He had not seen her. In the dusk he passed so close that she could hear the catch of his breath.

She did not look up. Pressing her hands to her bandaged breasts, she whispered, "He'll never want me now." It was not Set she meant. "Nobody will."

When Set was gone she stood up, remembering the words of the bear ceremony: *"I am spirit without place."*

Life was as pointless to hold on to as the mug of tea. Turning, she walked north into the Tells, the place of spirits.

She went straight up and over the first low hill, and Creek disappeared behind her.

She was surrounded by stone: square blocks from fallen chimneys, smashed flagstones, the triangular keystones of ruined arches. Stones teetered and sprawled, leaning in lines once straight. Scrawny, vigorous weeds elbowed up among them.

She did not look at anything. As though late to a rendezvous she hurried on.

Potsherds crackled underfoot. Kat paused. Broken pottery paved the dirt like shining gravel.

She bent; she picked up one shard after another as if they were money, tipping them in the dimming light.

Some were painted with the same designs—the Bear's Eye, the Trout, the Creek—that Kat had learned last summer in the potting shed. Others were left unglazed to show the mica glitter of the clay, and drawings of animals were carved into them.

Because the pots were broken, the animals were broken too. Kat found half a deer, the ears of a rabbit, a lizard's head. Carved around each animal were the tracks it made: the deer's heart shape, the seated rabbit's long foot, the lizard's dragging tail.

Kat picked up a shattered mug by its handle. Remembering that other broken mug, she dropped it; then she picked it up again.

It was carved with the track of the deer mouse, like the print of four fingers bunched together. The body of the mouse was lost, all but the tip of its tail.

"Everything is smashed," she said. She clenched her fist on the shard until it hurt her. That felt right. She dropped the broken mug into the pocket of her pinafore.

At her voice a jackrabbit zigzagged away, flashing its turkey-feather ears. Kat followed it over the next hillock. The air grew darker around her, as though night rose out of the ground.

Up a stony hummock, down into a corrie, up and down she walked among the dead stone houses.

How quiet, she thought. How still.

Suddenly the sun, at the horizon, shot under the roof of cloud. The hummocks were tipped with eerie light, the dells shadowy. Kat slithered into a little hollow that was like cupped hands.

At the very bottom of it a rosebush grew.

It was the same kind that trailed over the doorways of Creek. This bush was scruffy and small, struggling up between a heap of stones and a badger's burrow. Years of dead stems choked it, yet it was alive. It bore three withered rose hips.

Kat knelt and pulled one. It was wrinkled, dull red. She chewed it, puckering. Looking down, she saw beside her knee a woman's grinding stone.

She recognized it at once. She had used an identical stone, Bian's, to grind pigment to paint her water jar. It was lens-shaped, of black basalt, a handspan wide.

She picked it up. It was heavy, as though it did not want to leave the ground. The badger had scrabbled it to the surface as he dug his burrow, for the fresh dirt on it was scored with claw marks.

Kat spat on the flat surface and rubbed it with the hem of her pinafore. The grinding plane gleamed black, sleek as a mirror. In it Kat saw her own face, a ghost with hair of smoke instead of fire.

Someone else knelt here, Kat thought. Did she go up Dark Heart to her bear? Now she's dead. They buried her at her threshold with her stone, and planted this rosebush.

She thought of the roots groping down into the woman's flesh.

She had eaten the rose hip.

She sat back onto her heels, as though to pull her body out of a place that belonged to someone else's, and as she did she saw the woman herself.

A brown skull tilted on the badger's mound, freshly exhumed, staring. Around it lay scattered finger bones, vertebrae, a grinning mandible.

The tunnel from which they had been dragged drove deep under the roots of the rose. It was round-mouthed, with a darkness like suction, like the eyes of the bear.

Like the eyes of the bear the tunnel grew larger, blacker. From the terror that locked her eyes and breath Kat thought, That's death. I'll go to that. It'll be easier than the bear.

Her body made a short lurch forward.

But the broken mug in her pocket stabbed her knee; as at the ceremony, she tore her eyes from the tunnel with a cry and hit out—hit nothing, rolled away, her pinafore snagged in the rosebush.

She ripped it free. Blundering forward, directionless with fear, she ran out of the hollow—up the hill, down again, up and down, farther and farther from Creek.

The brown skeleton clattered behind her.

She heard it.

With a scream she raced faster, burst over the crest of a hill, ran straight into a man's chest, and knocked him sprawling.

He leaped to his feet like a cat shaken from a branch. Whipping around to face her where she crouched snarling, he cried, "Take me! I'm not afraid!"

He was not looking at her but past her, at the thing behind her. She wrenched herself around. There was nothing—nothing but the Tells wild with sunset and the bending grass.

"It's gone!" She hugged her breasts, sick with pain. "It's gone."

Still he looked beyond her. "Gone? What?" He rubbed his hand across his eyes. "Who the devil?"

It was Raím.

In the last blink of sun he blazed like a torch. He clenched his fists over his face and cried, "It's a *child*. Some rotten child, not death at all!"

"*I am not some rotten child!*" Kat screamed. "You . . . you *blind* man!"

His head jerked back. He lunged at her.

She scrambled up, skipped downhill beyond his reach. "Blind man!" she taunted, to avenge her terror. "Blind man!"

He groped, panting, in the direction of her voice; he caught his foot and fell to his knees. Clinging to a rock, he shouted, "Yes, I *am* blind!"

She came back into herself, sane and horrified. "I didn't mean it! I'm sorry!"

"Shut up," he said. "I know you now. You're the one the bear wouldn't eat."

She sat down on a stone, her hands on her breasts. "Yes, I am."

"You're Kat."

She thought, He didn't call me Lisei.

Aloud she said, "You're Raím."

"Who else?"

41

"What are you doing here?"

"I live here. Somewhere around here." He ground his teeth. "I've lost myself, trying to tackle you."

"You live in the *Tells*?" But he was flesh and blood, with skinned knees.

"On the edge of them. It's quiet, damn it. What the devil are *you* doing here?"

She remembered. "*Did you see it?*"

"'See it,'" he said, mocking her. "Sure. I saw an army of bears. I saw Leaguemen, I saw mice. What do you think? I heard screaming, then you hit me. I thought you were . . . I thought . . ."

"There was something after me."

"What?"

Kat plucked at the hem of her pinafore.

After a long silence Raím said, "I don't know where I am. You have eyes; go to the top of a mound and look north. You'll see my bothy on the plain."

"I won't go up there! It's almost dark."

"Dark!" He laughed bitterly and got to his feet. "Are you afraid of that 'something'?"

"Yes."

He was much taller than she was. In the twilight his pale face was luminous. "*I'm* not afraid. Because I'd just as soon be dead. Find my damned stick, I dropped it. Give me your hand, and I'll come with you while you look."

Kat spotted the white aspen staff hanging in a clump of sage and made a dash for it. Raím took it without thanks. "Your hand," he said.

His hand was warm and hard. She listened for the creek. Putting the creek at her right shoulder she trudged with him up the slope until she could look out over the dusky plain.

"I see firelight in a window."

"Take me there."

He was surefooted but slow. When they were near enough to hear the rasp of the young poplars that served as windbreak to the stone hut he said, "I know where I am," and dropped her hand.

"Don't leave me!" She grabbed the back of his tunic.

From the direction of Dark Heart, wild dogs began their hunting wail.

"Come on, then. But don't yank at me." Raím found the door. It was unlocked. He grasped the iron handle; then he stopped.

"Wait," he said. "I can't let you in here. There's a loom."

5

"I can't come in?"

The wild dogs barked, very near.

"My great loom is here. You can't look on it."

"Isn't it in the Holds?" The dogs howled; she crowded against Raím's back. "Don't leave me outside!"

"Be quiet." He rubbed his eyes. Then he said, "I'll cover the loom. Turn your head."

She turned her head; Raím opened the door, slipped in, and began to shut it.

"Don't shut it!"

"The devil! Stay there; do you think I'd let a girl look on my loom?"

He shut the door against her. She heard him bar it and say, "It's only dogs. If they come into the dooryard just shout."

With a sob Kat put her back to the door. She stared into the dusk.

The night wind rose. The shapes of the sagebrush moved. Behind her she heard low curses, thuds, a dragging sound. She got colder and colder. From the bothy came a horrible, battering din that slowed and, finally, stopped.

At the edge of the dooryard she saw a crouching, slinking shape.

"*Raím!*"

The door opened. As she tumbled into the bothy Raím said sullenly, "Come in."

She crouched on the sandy floor, gasping, until she was sure nothing had come in with her. Then she raised her head and looked around.

The single room was round and low, with a clay stove on one wall. Everything was dirty. By the light of the open grate Kat saw an ashy hearth, a bed of piled skins with a spindle thrown down on it, two stools, and a smutty cook pot. There was a maze of equipment that was foreign to her: hanks, ropes, wheels, raw cotton in bags, a grimy fleece.

But more than half the room was not visible. A huge, scarred tarpaulin had been nailed to a roof beam as a curtain. In the draft from under the door it rose and fell as though it breathed.

It was torn and hung crookedly, but whatever lay beyond it was dark. Anyway she did not want to see it.

"I shouldn't be here!" Kat wrung her frozen hands.

"The devil, after all that! Go back outside!"

Raím sucked a bruised thumb. He had used the teakettle for a hammer; it stood on the stove now, full of dents. When Kat did not answer he said, as if ashamed, "If you're still frightened I'll make more fire."

She shivered and said nothing.

He scowled. "More fire, then."

He groped for the poker and thrust it among the half-burned logs. The flames blazed up. He held his hand to the heat.

"Come here." He motioned her closer.

She did not move.

"The devil, what can I do? Here's fire. I'll give you tea and bread. You're safe. It's not dark for you."

One tight breath escaped her, almost a sob.

He rubbed his eyes and swore. Turning away, he paced like a lion that knows the limit of its cage—but he tangled with the tarpaulin, which he had already forgotten.

"What!" he said, shoving his hands in front of his face. Then he pushed them into his sash as though that was what he had meant to do all along. With his back to her he demanded, "So what was chasing you out there?"

She was silent.

"You think I don't believe you?" He rubbed his eyes. In a surly voice he said, "Once when I walked on the Tells at evening I heard a baby cry. Just at my left shoulder. I heard it whimper, and then the mother sang,

> Eyes full of light,
> The hawk's eyes.
> Eyes full of dark,
> The owl's eyes.

"I put out my hand. There was nothing. Stone. But the song went on."

Whispering, Kat said, "When you were a baby, were you blind?"

"No."

As though released from a spell she said, "It was a skeleton after me. Brown bones. I saw the hole it came from. Her grinding stone, I touched it; I ate her rose hip." Kat huddled close to the fire. "She wanted me to be dead like her. I ran. She followed me."

"Did you want to be dead?"

"No!"

"*I* wanted to be dead. When I heard that baby. I called the dead to me, wanting them."

"*Why?*"

"Why do you think?" He turned; his shoulders were very broad against the rotten tarpaulin. "I was a hunter once."

She looked at him, aware of her looking. He did not shut his useless eyes.

She knew she was blushing, and that he did not know it. "I did want to die," she said. "I wanted to die because of the bear."

He held out his hand to her.

Then he stopped himself, made a fist, and jeered. "Because of a little bear!"

He turned away, laid his hands accurately on the two stools, and pulled them to the fire. "Sit down," he said.

She sat.

He brought pine nuts, smoked rabbit, and bread, and shared it out between them. Kat could not eat. Raím ate deftly, cracking the bones for the marrow.

The canvas sighed and shook. Kat jumped; but it was only a wiry tabby tom, slipping from the shadows to watch each bite.

"Set hunts for me now," Raím said with his mouth full. "My brother. But I do all the rest. I don't need anybody. I built this house."

Kat offered the tom a hunk of meat, and he settled down to worry it.

"Don't feed the cat," said Raím. "He's to keep the mice down. There was an old house here before, all fallen in. It was easy to fix. I laid up the stones and chinked them." He scowled. "Set helped with the roof. Even a sighted man needs help with a roof." He turned his head. "I've never seen this place. So what? I get around fine. It's like being in a cave too deep for light."

Kat shuddered. "I don't like caves."

"That's because you're afraid of the dark."

She gave the rest of her smoked rabbit to the cat and said coldly, "I like to use my eyes."

His voice went mocking. "In a cave, eyes are no good. When the torch is gone there's nothing. You fight the bear in the dark. I've done that."

"When you *used to be* a hunter?"

"When I was the best hunter in Creek. When I brought every girl her bear."

"The bear they brought me was little. Like a dog."

"I would have brought you a big one." His smile was lazy, baiting. "You'd have run away from it, too, but at least you'd have had good reason."

She stood up and hit him with her fist, hard, right under the eye.

He sprawled backward with a crash. The tom fled behind the curtain.

Raím sat up slowly, his hand to his face. Kat took a stumbling half step toward the door. He made no move to rise. He pulled his hand away, and blood poured from his nose.

"Oh, no," she said. "I'm sorry. . . ."

"The devil! Why should you be sorry? Bring me the water bucket by the door."

"But you're blind. You couldn't see it coming." She hefted the bucket to him, splashing.

"I could see that coming without eyes. There's a rag somewhere—look on the nail by the stove. Give it to me."

"Tip your head back. It won't stop bleeding until you tip your head back."

He tipped his head back. She held his nose squeamishly with the rag, but he jerked away and chanted,

> Hunter, cudgel,
> Woman, bear.
> Show me your claws!
> Show me your red hair!

"That's a hunting song. I have claw scars on my back; this is more blood than that was. You hit like a man."

"I'm not a man."

"Neither am I. A man hunts bears." He wiped his nose on his wrist and took the rag from her. "Why are you still here? I insulted you, you hit me. Go."

"It's dark out."

"That's not why. You stay because if you don't fix me up again I'll think you're mannish. Men make things bleed, women fix them." He spat into the bucket. "I've said I'm not a man. You don't have to stay to prove you're a woman."

She said, "I'm a woman whether I stay or go." She sat down again. The cat came angling back, and she took him onto her lap. "But you can hold your own nose. It won't kill you."

Pressing the rag to his face, Raím groped for his stool and set it upright.

"Where I was born," said Kat, "men don't hunt bears. They don't weave. Men make money, and women clean house. Then there's another place I know, where the men fish and cook, and the women sell the fish to make money." She raked the tabby's back with her fingers. "When I came to Creek I thought it was very strange, all this about bears."

"But you went to your bear."

Suddenly tears were there, a storm of them. "I wanted to be a woman of the Circle!" said Kat. "I wanted to be beautiful and ordinary and have a lover."

Raím cursed. He reached out as though to touch her knee, then withdrew his hand. "You women cry all the time. Stop crying. Creek means nothing, all its ceremonies and bears."

"Nothing? The way you talk, the bear hunt is your manhood!"

He wiped the last of the blood from his face. "My brother is my manhood."

"But you still hide your loom."

"Every man since Trouble . . . ," said Raím. Then, "So what if I'm not a man! This is my house, I can do what I want."

The tom leaped to the floor, sniffed Raím's bloody wrist, and began to lick it.

Outside the wild dogs sang. Kat shivered. "It's late."

"I'll take you back. Night or day, the path is the same to me."

"But—the wild dogs?"

"What about them?"

"They'll attack us!"

"The hell they will. They're little, like your bear. They'd steal a child, if they could catch one." Raím shrugged. "But you're not a child."

Kat drew a deep breath. "Please take me home, then."

"You won't want to come back here." Raím turned his head away. "You should come back. The cat likes you."

"What's his name?"

"Brook."

"Brookie," she said, and the tom came to lean against her shins.

Raím stood up. His eye was swelling shut. "Oh, leave the damned cat. You'll get me in trouble for keeping you out."

"You're not keeping me."

"According to the gossips in Creek?" He flung another log into the stove; firelight blazed up on the torn canvas. He stuck out his hand. She took it.

Outside the clouds had blown away in patches to show the starry Hunter falling, falling in the west. As Kat shut the door behind them Raím said suddenly, "What you said. About wanting to be beautiful. You stupid woman!" He turned his blind, bitter face toward her in the starlight. "You're fine."

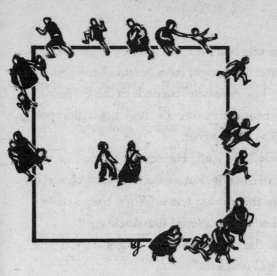

6

THE MORNING WAS BRIGHT, and the sky outside the open door was full of rushing clouds. Jekka washed the breakfast dishes. Mamik swung on the door handle, half hiding, peeking at Kat until Bian scolded him, "Get along to your father. I don't want that cold wind on my bread."

She turned to Kat, trouble deepening on her face. "You were with Raím?"

"I got lost on the path by the creek."

Kat wished she had said nothing about Raím. He had left her as soon as she could see the east gate; the rest of the family had been out when she got back to the house, and they might have been none the wiser.

To hide her face she turned to hug Mamik. Before the bear ceremony he had been her pet, affectionate as a baby goat.

"Get away," he said. He squirmed out of her arms and ran outside. Kat saw a crowd of children craning over the garden fence. When they saw her they squeaked and scattered like ducklings.

She shut the door and said, "It got dark. I saw light in Raím's window."

"*There?* You didn't go in?" So Bian knew there was a loom.

"Raím was outside," said Kat, looking at her hands.

"If I'd known! You with those wounds. We heard wild dogs!" Bian was kneading bread, thumping it hard between breaths. "Raím. A pity. A strong lad. He was wild. But they're all wild. Men. When they're young." She slapped the dough down and dusted her hands. "That's their nature. Even my Emmot was rowdy, just like Set. Set will make a good man when he settles down, but Raím—he's wild with pain, we all know it. Cub, he's not someone I like to see you with."

"He only brought me home."

"I'm glad of that, sister's daughter."

"My name is Kat."

"Kat, then! Only have a little wisdom. You must prove to Creek that you are not cursed. That means you must walk a narrow path of obedience until you come safe into the mouth of the Mother. Would it further you to be seen with Raím?"

"What's the matter with him?"

"The matter! The boy is blind."

"That's only sad. It's not wicked."

"Well, I can't say," said Bian. "Who's to know?"

"Who's to know what? You think he's cursed? What did he *do*?"

Bian put her fists on her hips. "Thank Ouma, you're feeling better! But I don't like this back talk."

Jekka spoke over her shoulder from the dishpan. "*I* think Raím was cursed for being too good-looking. He used to be handsomer than Set. We called him Torch—he was always fighting and singing, in trouble over some girl. Wenta would scream across the plaza, 'You shameless lout!' and he'd laugh! You could hear Raím's laugh clear across Creek." She glanced slyly at her mother. "And could he dance! We prayed to go to our bears so we could dance with Raím."

"Tcha!" said Bian. She flapped a clean dishcloth over the bread. "Ouma's ways are mysterious, and I assure you, the older you get the more mysterious they seem. Who knows why the Mother took Raím's sight?"

"Ouma struck his eyes out?" said Kat.

"He fell," said Jekka. "The men were hunting on the cliffs. Raím leaped to a rock, it turned under his foot, and he fell into the chasm where it's too steep to climb. It took the men a day to get to him. For a month he didn't move, didn't speak." Jekka shuddered. "I'm sure he's cursed. His eyes were fine— nothing touched them—but when he woke he was blind."

"That was an accident," said Kat. "That could happen to anybody!"

"I'm not the judge," said Bian. "What I know is that, even blind, Raím is a fine weaver. There would be a place for him inside the walls if he'd have it— but he won't have it. He hides on the Tells, of all places, and won't tolerate anyone but his brother to see to him. I can imagine what a sty that bothy must be. Cub, it's a virtue to let your neighbors help you. Why should Raím skulk outside the walls, like a Leagueman or a wild dog?"

In a low voice Kat said, "Maybe he's ashamed that he can't hunt anymore."

"He won't accept that he's blind. It's male pride." Bian's voice was both fond and bitter. "Men! When they're little they're like us. But kittens grow to be cats. Boys get big; they get proud and wild, and unless we tame them they take, take, whatever they want. My Mamik, I'll lose him soon, as surely as I buried the others."

"All men aren't like that," said Kat, thinking, Not my Nall!

"Say what you will," said Bian. "A man not tamed by a woman of the Circle is no better than a Leagueman. And who'll tame Raím now? Not you, my cub." She rubbed her hand along Kat's cheek, leaving a floury mark. "Oh, if I could guard you in my heart! You're so young and naked, sister's daughter."

"Kat."

"Kat! Kat!" Bian laughed. "I swear, it would be easier to eat you myself, and have it over with. What a bellyache you'd give me! Don't have anything to do with Raím, lovey. It looks bad."

"It's Set she's sweet on," said Jekka.

"I am not!"

"Well, Set's normal as daylight," said Bian. "Bless

him! He's who Raím should have been. But even so, Kat, tell me this: what was the name of Ouma's husband?"

"Trouble."

"That's all you need to know about men. Come here. Give me a hug, and let me see your hurt."

"I do feel better."

"You look *much* better," said Jekka, taking off her apron. "Why don't you come with me to the Clay Court?"

"I don't want to." Kat thought of the children scrambling away from the fence. "No."

"Sooner or later you'll have to," said Jekka. "You can't sit at home for the rest of your life."

"She'll show me those wounds before she goes anywhere," said Bian. "There! I thought a walk would do you good. That one is dry, and maybe that one. Praise the Mother, what scars you'll have!" She folded a fresh linen bandage and fastened it with the brass pin. "But the tattoos will cover them. The Circle has decided: the hunters will bring another bear for you. But not until you're ready. You must ask for it."

With her head bent Kat said, "Till then, will people mind if I walk on their streets?"

"Oh, my hurt baby!" said Bian. "Sister's child!"

"Kat."

Jekka said, "If anybody bothers you I'll punch them. Do come with me, cousin. You should start making another water jar, for when you go to your bear."

Bian raised Kat's face in her hands. With a loving, searching look she said, "Dear daughter, there's nothing I want more than your happiness. If anything troubles you, you'll tell me?"

Kat thought of the forbidden loom and squirmed like Mamik. "I love you, Bian." To escape her aunt's eyes she said, "Jekka, I *will* come with you."

"I knew you would! Get your satchel. I'll make us lunch."

They went out the gate and down the street toward the Clay Court. Kat lagged behind. The wind brought the smell of damp dirt and the yell of birds. It seemed as though everyone in Creek was in the street, hauling a market basket or bustling on some spring errand with a hoe or a tub of onion sets. The crowd jostled and chatted—except around Kat and Jekka. There, voices fell silent and the crowd opened to let them pass. A woman with a baby on her hip turned the child's face away; Jekka stuck out her tongue, but with her own face ducked so that no one but Kat could see.

There were no nods, no smiles. No one said "Good morning." In a magic circle of silence, with plenty of elbow room, Kat and Jekka crossed the square.

"Ignorant clods," said Jekka. "I'm glad they won't talk. It would be all stupidities. Your conversation's better. Say something."

"What?" said Kat. She was watching her feet. If she looked up she saw the Bear House, or eyes.

"Anything, ninny. *Ask* me something."

Kat wished she were blind; then she wished everyone else were. She said, "When did he fall?"

"Who? Oh, Raím. Four years ago, right before my bear. I cried, because I couldn't dance with him after all."

As she spoke, Jekka's voice had quickened. Kat looked at her, then glanced around.

Esangi walked under the rose trees on the shadow side of the square.

Her pale hair was tightly braided and pinned under a scarf, and her wiry arms ended in fists. Her lip was swollen, and her stare, unlike those of the rest of Creek, was direct and hard. Mía walked with her, hanging back.

"Let's walk faster," said Jekka. Kat complied with a jump, as if she had been pinched. At a trot they started down the colonnade, under the bare trees.

Near the granaries they looked back. Esangi was strolling faster too, with a taunting look, and Mía was puffing to keep up.

Kat and Jekka dove into a crowd of marketers, who scrambled to get out of their way. Jekka grabbed Kat's arm, yanked her into a narrow alley beside an outhouse, and hustled her down a weedy path that smelled of garlic and slops.

"I think," said Jekka, "that if nobody wants to talk to us we'll just take another route."

They ducked behind woodsheds and under wash lines, startling a fat woman who stopped chopping wood and fled with a squeal. After many turnings they came out on the south side of town through a little gate beside the goat pens.

"It might be a good idea," said Jekka, not meeting Kat's eyes, "to be sure Sisira is at the potting shed before we go there. Nobody fights when Sisira's at the shed."

"I can't run anymore." Kat pressed one hand to the bandages.

"Then stay here a minute. I'll go ahead and make sure Sisira's there. If anybody comes by, slide around back of that haystack and they won't see you."

Jekka left. The wounds burned. Kat leaned against a gatepost. She could not get out of her mind the image of Raím, lying broken on the rocks.

Something nudged her thigh—it was Zella's wicked old billy, sticking his bearded chin through the bars of the fence. He was ugly and muscular and he stank, but Kat rubbed him between his slotted yellow eyes. It was good to be stared at by someone who only wanted his head scratched. She offered him corn bread from her satchel.

"Don't waste lunch on that gross beast," said Jekka, returning. "All he's good for is running off so somebody has to run after him. Sisira's at the shed, cousin. It'll be all right."

"Are you sure?"

"Positive."

"*Me-e-eh,*" said Zella's goat.

7

THEY CAME INTO the Clay Court by the south gate, under the stone lintel that men could not cross. The sandy yard, scarred with the ash of old firings and scattered with potsherds, was empty. Jekka pushed open the door of the main shed.

The shed was chilly as a cave and smelled like damp clay. Wooden workbenches stood in herds like horses with their noses together; racks held a cluster of unfinished pots; on a shelf the ranks of grinding stones shone dully. The black tile stove in the middle of the room was cold.

"Mother's peace," said Sisira the clay keeper, coming out of the shadows by the drying shelves. "Good morning, Lisei's daughter."

She did not look at Kat's eyes as she spoke but at her breasts, at the bandages that the blouse and pinafore did not quite cover.

Kat put up one hand as though to hide them. "Peace."

"I'm glad to see you back at your learning," said Sisira. As she spoke she made the hand sign against cursing, her fingers half-hidden. "Wake the fire," she said, and moved away to the far side of the shed.

Kat stooped before the stove. She knew how to wake a fire. But that chant, like the words of all ceremonies, had fled her. She whispered to Jekka, "What do I say?"

"*Wake, wake,* ninny," Jekka whispered back. She dumped her satchel on a bench. "I'm going to teach you so well that you'll never forget. Watch. I stir the ashes. I put the smallest kindling on last night's coals, and blow—see it catch? Then bigger wood. Then I say, *Wake, wake, day's fire*—Kat! Don't turn around, there's somebody at the door. Let me handle it."

But it was only Mamik, sniffing into the potting shed like a little dog, tossing his spindle.

Indignant, Jekka said, "What are you doing, baby, bringing your spindle in here?"

"I forgot." Mamik gave Kat a sidelong glance and ran to lay his spindle outside. He sidled back, ducked behind Jekka, and leaned on her. "I'm cold. Mía says I'm too big to be in here. I'm not, am I?" He stared at Kat from under his sister's elbow. "Jekka, is our cousin cursed?"

"Of course not. Where did you hear that silliness?"

"The kids."

"The kids are stupid."

"The big girls say it too. They say she'll be like Raím, she'll get blind and crazy and walk on the Tells."

"The *girls* are crazy. Kat's not cursed." Jekka thought for a moment. "She gets two tries."

"Oh." Mamik looked doubtful. "In cudgelball we get three. Give me raisins, Jekka."

Jekka scratched in her satchel. "Here. Go back to Father. We're girls, we don't want you." When Mamik was gone Jekka gave Kat a firm, loyal squeeze. "After you go to your bear I'm going to give you my green glass necklace."

Kat said nothing, but two tears splashed on her wrist.

"Mamik loves you. Really. He just has to see that you're all right." Jekka tossed an extra log into the stove and wiped her forehead. "So does everybody, Kat. You should do the marketing for Mother, and go to the dances. People would see you and get used to you. You might get to know Set better, too. It wouldn't matter about the scars."

Kat was not listening. She rose, stepping half behind her cousin. Esangi and Mía came through the shed door, their clogs crackling in the dry clay scraps. Selem and Bo followed, so timidly that they appeared to lean backward as they walked.

"Mother's peace," said Mía, nodding to Sisira.

"Peace."

"We waited till the fire was hot." Mía's voice was placid, but her eyes, like the eyes of the rest, were on Kat's breasts. She cleared her throat and asked, "How are you, Kat?"

"I'm all right."

"Speak up," said Esangi. "*We* won't eat you, baby cub."

Selem and Bo tittered. Sisira coughed. Mía said, "It was a pleasure to hear that you're to stay in Creek. We missed you in our Circle."

"She's not in our Circle. She's a cub." Esangi

pushed forward to warm her hands, and the other girls fell back. They always seemed to defer to her fierce certainties, as if they feared or pitied her.

"We're all daughters of the Mother," said Mía.

"She's her Leagueman daddy's daughter."

Kat heard Jekka mutter under her breath, "You're no daddy's daughter at all."

"What?" said Esangi.

"I said, if you bother my cousin at all you're dog's meat."

"Jekka!" said Sisira.

Jekka shrugged. Esangi, glaring, threw her satchel onto a wall bench and went to fetch her grinding stone.

The other girls whispered among themselves. Bárteme, Sara, and Elanne came in, sneaking glances at Kat and making the hand sign. It was always the unmarried girls, with no children to tend, who came first to the sheds.

Jekka herded Kat toward the low wooden benches that Emmot had built for both of them. Kat's was newer, but already it was grimy with good use. Kat had enjoyed potting; she liked the shifting liveliness of the wet clay. Before the bear she had begun to think, Maybe someday I could make something besides a water jar. Something of my own.

Now, as she straddled the bench and settled her knees into the notches, she remembered the kindliness of work. It surprised her that she could feel a little glad.

Jekka brought her a wad of clay. "You're coming along fine," she said, loudly enough for the others to hear. "But you've been gone for a while; you'll have to get back into it slowly. Practice making a water jar, of course. Tell me the clay chant."

"*Under my hand*," Kat began, and remembered the whole thing.

Satisfied, Jekka left her. The room settled to a working quiet, warmed slowly by the stove. Every now and then one of the girls would stare at Kat, or a pair of them would whisper.

Kat did not notice. She wedged her lump of clay. As she rocked back and forth, leaning her weight onto the heels of her hands, she remembered the first thing she had ever heard in the Hill tongue: a lullaby that her mother had sung.

> Bear in the black rock,
> Bear's two children.

My red cub, O!
My brown cub, O!

It made her think of the lullaby the ghost had sung to Raím on the Tells. From the pocket of her pinafore she fished out the shard with the deer-mouse track and laid it in front of her on the potting bench.

Her hands felt soft and crackly with dried slip. She rolled out the first thin snake of clay and began to build her water jar, winding and pinching the coil into a base.

The shed grew hot. Someone opened the door onto the yard, letting in the vigorous wind. Kat did not notice. Pinch and turn, pinch and turn, her hands corrected the shape as the clumsy bowl rose.

It did not want to be a water jar. It was much too small. It almost made itself, round as cupped hands, with a little lip.

I know what it is! Kat thought. It's a pot to hold wild honey.

She turned it in her hands, using a gourd-skin scraper to smooth away her fingerprints and thin the walls.

Peaceful as a leaf floating on a lake, she thought

about the ivory seal, its catlike glance hidden in the honeycomb. That made her think of Brook, then of Raím.

He'd like pottery that wasn't all smoothed and painted, she thought. Or pots with designs carved into them. There'd be more for him to *feel*.

She looked at the red potsherd from the Tells. Its surface was rough and lively.

She picked up a splinter of kindling from the unswept floor and dragged it along the shoulder of the pot. But the clay was already hardening; the splinter left only a shallow, ugly scratch.

She thought. Her belt knife would be too clumsy, her fingernail too dull. At last she put her hands to her neck, unfastened the brass pin that secured the bandages, and tucked in the ends of the cloth so they would not slip. She bent the pin until its scoop-shaped guard stuck out.

It made a perfect carving tool. Looking at the potsherd, Kat cut a trail of hopping tracks, forepaw and hind paw, and the flick of a tail. It was easy, like drawing in sand. Then she began to carve the deer mouse.

Delicate whiskers spread under her hand, tiny ears sprouted like corn kernels, a plump body appeared with its balancing tail. Like the seal's eyes, like Brook's, the mouse's eyes were sharp and wild.

Kat laughed out loud. "Jekka!" she said. "Come look!"

But it was not Jekka who came. It was Esangi, carrying a painted bowl to the drying rack. She stood an arm's length away.

"What's that?" she said. "What are you doing?"

All heads in the potting shed bobbed up, all eyes stared.

"You're supposed to be making a water jar for the bear. What's this thing? And you're supposed to be learning the signs and rites—what sign is that?"

"It's a mouse," said Kat. "A deer mouse."

"We're not mice! We're bears. Where's the Bear's Eye sign?"

"I didn't make that."

Sisira had gone out for firewood; she was not in the shed.

Esangi set down her painted bowl.

Mía said, "What's the matter, Esangi?"

"She's ruining the pots. Where's the Bear's Eye? Does this rotten cub want to be eaten by a mouse? She didn't want to be eaten by the bear!"

"Of course she wanted to," said Mía in her most

official voice. She rose to look, as Jekka, with a face of thunder, crossed the room from the drying shelves. "I mean, she *will* want to, next time. The Circle says—"

"The Circle says she can fool around being a child as long as she feels like it. She'll never be a woman. She's afraid to, because she knows her daddy hated them." Esangi brought her thin face down close to Kat's. "I wanted to be a woman, Leagueman's brat. I wanted to be eaten by the bear from the day my mother bore me."

Kat stammered, "I hardly remember my mother."

"Only your daddy."

Jekka said, "Leave her alone!"

"You can't live here and not be eaten by the bear," said Esangi. "We'll drive you out, like a Leagueman. Like a wild dog."

"Kat escaped to us!" said Jekka. "She ran away from the Leaguemen!"

"They're dogs." Esangi gave Kat a flat, bright smile. "They rape women. We hate them. Brat, do you hate your father?"

"He was cruel. He never liked me."

"*Do you hate him?*"

At that instant Kat could only think of her father miserable with a cold: sneezing, both feet in mustard water. She said, "I don't know."

"He's a dog! You have to hate him if you want to be one of us."

"Esangi. Sister."

It was Sisira. She had been standing at the door, her arms full of firewood. Coming close, she said in a neutral voice, "Kat can't learn right if we don't teach her."

"Did we teach her that?" Esangi pointed. "It's the mouse that steals our corn. And we say the paintbrush is Ouma's tongue, she licks her cubs with it. So why is this cub scratching the pots with a pin? And look! That potsherd's from the Tells!"

The girls murmured. Esangi said, "She'll bring a curse on us. I'll break that pot!" She snatched a stick of wood from the pile in Sisira's arms and raised it.

"No!" Kat half rose, spreading her hands to protect the mouse.

The unpinned bandages slipped down to show the damp scabs, hideous as burns.

Esangi lowered the stick. "You're tattooed, all

right," she said. She threw the log into the stove. "If you ever got a man he could feel them, even if he was blind."

She turned and left the shed.

"I'll kill her!" Jekka blundered after her through the benches. Mía blocked her way. Kat stood motionless.

Sisira touched her shoulder. "Sit, cub."

Kat sat.

"Half-wrongs are half-rights," said Sisira. "We could wish the past had been different for Esangi— or for Esangi's mother."

"Damn Esangi!" said Jekka. "She'd better leave Lisei alone!"

"The Leaguemen didn't leave Lisei alone," said Sisira. "What Esangi said is true. Leaguemen rape women."

"I didn't mean Lisei. I meant Kat."

Kat said, "My father didn't rape my mother. She went with him because she loved him."

"You don't know that!" said Jekka, ready to lay her anger anywhere.

"They raped somebody," said Sisira. "On the road to Ten Orchards. That's why we drove the

Leaguemen out of Creek. And if anyone has a right to remark upon it, it's Esangi."

To Kat she said, "Lisei's daughter. It was wrong to take a potsherd from the Tells. Those women went up Dark Heart without guidance; they angered Ouma, and I think it's not wise to study their ways. It was wrong to make a toy when you must learn to make a water jar. It was wrong to wound the clay with a pin."

Sisira dumped her armload of wood by the stove. "I'll speak to Esangi. If necessary, Wenta the headwoman will speak to her as well. Now, cub—put the potsherd in your pocket and throw it back on the Tells. And destroy that pot. There's no lack of pretty things to make that are also good things—moral and useful. Maybe, after you are safely one of us, you may experiment, in Ouma's name."

"Give me the pot," said Jekka. "We can use that clay for something else."

Kat surrendered her work. She fumbled to replace the brass pin.

"Let me do that."

It was Mía. She took the pin, bent it back into shape, and repinned the bandages. She looked over the other girls with her calm, managing gaze. "We'll all help you, won't we? Cub, come sit by me. I'll teach you to paint the Bear's Eye sign."

"I already know it," said Kat. But she sat by Mía's elbow for the rest of the morning.

"Sit still," said Jekka. "If you let me brush your hair *hard*, it'll grow fast, and you'll look more normal."

In nightgowns, the cousins sat alone by the hearth in front of the fine mirror that Emmot had bought at the shop in Ten Orchards. Sparks flew from the brush, and Kat's hair crackled and shone. Jekka said, "Set was hanging around under our window this afternoon. Mother chased him off."

"He likes you, *ow!*" said Kat as her curls were yanked.

She was exhausted. There was clay grit under her fingernails, and wherever she looked she saw the Bear's Eye sign: carved into the mantel, stamped into the tin of the bellows, embroidered along the edge of Jekka's sleeve.

"Not me! I'm too much like him—nice ankles and a big mouth. He's after somebody sweeter, and I know who."

"Who?"

"Ninny! You, of course."

Kat jerked her head away. "He is not! Nobody else will even *look* at me!"

Jekka cuffed her with the brush. "You flap worse than Mamik. Why shouldn't Set be interested? You're pretty, cousin."

"I'm not pretty."

"You are. Besides, that man's so brassy, if the village disapproves of something he has to do it right away. He loves to rush in where it's dangerous. Not that you're actually dangerous," Jekka added hastily.

"He'd never want me," Kat whispered. "Not how I am."

"He likes small women. He used to court Sara, and she barely comes up to his armpit."

"I don't mean that!"

But Jekka said only, "It's mean how hard Set has to work. He hunts for his brother like a slave, and all he gets is sworn at. Be nice to him, Kat. He's good-looking, and besides, he's Wenta's grandson."

She gave Kat's curls a final swipe. "There! My arm's tired." She pulled a shining nest of hair from the brush and laid it on the coals. "Time to bank the fire. I'll give you one last lesson."

79

Kat sighed, watching the hair wither and smoke.

Jekka picked up the tongs. "You know this. It's just like this morning. I bank the fire, so. I draw the circle in the ashes, and I sing,

> Sleep, sleep, day's fire,
> Bold, bright, brave!
> Ashes be your cradle
> That might have been your grave.

"Then in the morning I sing, *Wake, wake,* and the day's set right. Ouma holds all of it tight and takes care of everything." Jekka clattered the tongs back into the rack. "You didn't do anything like that in your old land?"

"Not really."

"No ceremony for bread? For planting corn?"

Kat shook her head.

"It's a wonder you're not frozen or starved. Or naked. Those foreign men don't weave, do they?"

"No. They buy cloth."

"That's just some stranger's cloth. Our men weave for us. Well, they trade at Ten Orchards too, but that doesn't count. Weaving's their mystery, but they do it for their women."

Kat wondered what woman Raím was weaving

for. She thought of the night sky over the Tells, wide as the ocean.

"Come to bed," said Jekka, yawning. "Mamik's snoring like a teakettle already."

"In a minute."

"It'll have to be. I'll be asleep in two. I told Mother we'd practice the bear songs."

"You said banking the fire was the last lesson!"

"I promised Mother. Besides—I'm going to *make* you learn. I'll show that Esangi! I'm going to make you perfect, and get you safe."

"Jekka, I'll be right in. I left my clogs in the garden. Some town dog will carry them off."

"Ninny! Well, poke me when you come to bed." Jekka trailed off to the bedroom, pulling out hairpins, her long braid uncoiling like a snake.

Kat slipped out the front door, shut it, and leaned on it.

The night was cold and still. Stars hung close and enormous in the bowl of heaven.

Cringing on her bare feet, she ran down the flagstone walk. She laid her forearms on the gate and leaned her cheek on them. The houses of Creek stood against the sky like rocks at the sea's edge. How lonely the ocean of stars!

On the Tells the wild dogs began to wail. Raím would be hearing them. Aloud Kat said, "*He* must be lonely."

"He is."

She jumped back, away from the voice.

Set leaned his arms on the gate where hers had been. "Cubby, are you scared?"

She groped for Jekka's insults. "This cub has claws! This cub . . . This cub . . ."

"You can't do it. You're so sweet it breaks my heart."

She stamped her foot. "Get off our gate!"

He pulled the spindle from his sash and twirled it down over the fence. His face was mischievous and mocking.

"You're different," he said. "Creek girls are all the same. Is it true that in your land women never go to the bear?"

"We don't need to."

"And women don't tattoo their breasts?"

"Why should you ask me! You saw!"

He leaned over the gate, leaned toward her. "Listen. I don't mind scars. I can show you scars— we'll trade. Is it true that in your land women have to do whatever men want?"

"No!"

He laughed. Like Mamik wheedling for raisins he said, "Come on, darling. One kiss. I like your chin."

She stalked to the house and let herself in, shut the door, and leaned on it.

The air was stuffy, full of kitchen smells.

"Ka-a-at!" came Jekka's wail. "I'm falling aslee-ee-eep!"

"I'm coming."

She pressed her palms to her eyes, then to her breasts; she started toward the bedroom.

She turned back. Taking up the brass lamp and the tongs, she searched for a coal to light the wick, spoiling the circle drawn on the ashes. Then she went to the fine Ten Orchards mirror, to look at her chin.

8

RAÍM BENT OVER the bucket next to the rain barrel, shirtless, washing his neck. The sun was warm, and the dew was rising off the new sage. He had pushed his kilt down low; from where Kat stood, motionless among the poplars, she could see around his hips the blue tattooed snake of his initiation.

She thought, He's Set's brother, so probably that's what Set looks like with his shirt off.

Raím squinted his eyes against the soap like any man, and sang,

> Green grass, morning,
> I see you, I see.
> White sun, noonday,
> I see you, I see.
> Red rock, sunset,
> I see you, I see.

He poured hot water from the kettle and began to shave, mirrorless, meticulous.

As a small child Kat had watched her father shave. Later he had banished her, embarrassed by her eyes, but she remembered the smell of the soap. Now, unseen and fascinated, she watched Raím.

He wiped the razor on his thigh. Her glance slid to the bothy door. It was open; in its shadows a square shape was almost visible.

An impulse to look at the forbidden loom drew her one step out of the poplars. Then she saw Brook sitting by the doorway, his huge gold eyes watching her as she watched.

She did not know where to look.

Noiselessly she withdrew behind the trees, back down the path. When she was out of earshot she sat down on a tussock of dry grass and said, "Stupid nosy cat!"

It was more than two weeks since the Circle had met to decide what to do about Kat. Bian must have argued well, for the fear of Kat's curse had seemed to ease a little, except among the mothers of the smallest babies. In trade for this acceptance, however, the Circle was unanimous: Kat must be taught, and taught thoroughly, how to be a woman of Creek.

Bian taught her the baking chants. Jekka sang the bear songs. Sisira watched as Kat made water jar after water jar, none perfect enough. Mía taught and retaught the Bear's Eye sign, the Trout, the Creek; the other girls showed her how to wedge clay, clean paintbrushes, and use the grinding stone.

Only Esangi did not teach. She was sullen and silent. She stopped all her common potting and began to make grain-storage jars.

They were a wordless boast. Enormous and thin-walled, they were horribly difficult to make. Damp clay collapsed, firm curves sagged, coils cracked in the drying. Only the most skilled older potters made them, and even then few jars survived the kiln.

But with uncanny patience Esangi built walls, saw them fall, built them again until they stood. The temper was too coarse; Esangi brought new clay from the creek bank. The coils cracked; Esangi smashed the pots and started over. She was first at the shed every morning, her hair pale in the firelight, her thin body tense with work.

She spoke to no one. Sometimes Kat sat next to her on purpose, because there she could be almost alone for a while, undisturbed by anything but hate.

At first Kat had been grateful for the other girls' attention and relieved to see the stares in the street grow less fearful. But then, as stout women came from the far side of the village to teach her how to plant corn, as grandmothers filled her evenings with endless important myths, and bossy children tried to teach her their jump-rope rhymes, she began to feel besieged. She avoided the marketplace. On the way to the Clay Court she kept to back alleys, hurrying, head down.

This was also to avoid Set. He was everywhere—teasing, cajoling, strolling with his friends. He did not call her name. He whistled, and when she turned he would be grinning, his thumbs in his belt. Kat could not even get a good look at him; his eyes were always on her first, impudent and challenging, and she had to look away.

It was annoying, and very flattering. Kat lay in

bed at night and wondered what he looked like with his shirt off.

This morning she had dreamed about him. In the dream he *had* taken his shirt off, and his chest was painted with hundreds and hundreds of Bear's Eye signs.

She had gotten up then. She put a half pan of corn bread in her leather sash pouch, told four different people that she would be in four different places, and slipped out alone along the path beside the creek. She did not want to run into Set, and she did not want to paint the Bear's Eye sign.

She had run like a dog let loose. Almost before she knew it she was passing the Tells.

Flinching, she remembered the skeleton. The potsherd knocked in her pocket; she had been so harried with lessons that there had been no time to come here and throw it back—or so she had told herself.

"I'll toss it on the way home," she said, and ran on past the Tells, onto the open plain.

Away to the left she saw the line of scrawny poplars that must be the windbreak for Raím's bothy. She had had no plan beyond getting out of Creek, but now she drifted toward the bothy, dawdling, picking sage to sniff. Finally she said, "Well, at least *he* can't stare back." Powerful in her invisibility, she had crept up on Raím's shaving ritual; then Brook had spoiled it all.

"Snoopy cat," she said, digging the heels of her clogs into the sand. She would walk to the quarry by the creek and gather clay instead. Sisira would be pleased with her, and anyway that was where she had told Mía she was going. Then she said, "Well. I'll thank Raím for bringing me home. Just to be nice."

She rose and returned to the bothy, scuffling loudly with her feet.

Raím scowled over the old shirt that he was using for a towel. "Subtle," he said. "Whoever you are. You want me to know you're coming, so you walk as if you'd stepped in dung."

"I'm leaving!" she said. "So there!"

"It's you!" He stepped forward. "Kat?"

She was silent, keeping her eyes away from the bothy door.

"It *is* Kat. I know your voice." He rubbed his eyes. The bruise around the left one was no longer black but a peculiar green. "You weren't coming back. I was sure."

"I wasn't afraid to!"

"Of course not. It's daytime." Then he raised his shoulders and said stiffly, "Look. I'm really rude. All the time."

"Yes, you are!"

"If you don't like it you can go."

"I didn't come to see you. I'm gathering clay." Too late, she realized that the clay was by the creek. "And I wanted to see this place by daylight."

"Oh," he said. "Well, here it is." He waved with his shirt, turning away.

There were long bear scars on the muscles of his back.

She put her hands to her breasts and said, "I did come to see you. But Bian doesn't want me to, and Jekka says you're cursed."

He turned slowly. She remembered that he had been called Torch—he burned, but not with brightness. "Speak," he said huskily. "Speak again, so I know where you are."

She stood still as a fawn.

"Oh, god!" He threw down the shirt. "I *am* cursed. Speak, speak! I won't hurt you." He put his hand to his eyes.

"I'm here," she said in a small voice, but when he stepped toward her she said, "Don't touch me!"

Like the bear in harness he swung his weight from foot to foot, swung his head. "Touch is all I have."

Brook sauntered over from the doorstep and pushed his face against Raím's legs. Raím scooped him up.

"Brook," he said. "Because he pours, like water. He has a life somewhere, apart from me. But I only know him when I can touch him." He tipped his hands and the cat leaped out of them. Raím said, "Go see the lady."

Brook pattered over to dust Kat's ankles with his whiskers.

Raím's mouth was almost soft—a handsome mouth. Kat said, "You're rude, it's repulsive."

"I like being repulsive."

He went to wash the last of the soap from his face. Over his shoulder he said, "Why doesn't Bian want you to see me?"

"Because you were wild."

"'Were'! My life around that word! I didn't feel half so wild as I do now, and it was better."

"Bian says you skulk outside the walls like a dog. She says your bothy is a sty."

"Since when was she in it, the bitch? Do you consult her about everything?"

91

"Bian knows about life. About men."

"Nobody knows about men. Not even men." Raím tugged his tunic over his head and knotted the sash. "I know only one thing about myself, and that's that I can't have what I want. Will you come skulk with me?"

"What?"

"Take a walk with me. I'll get my cursed stick. I won't touch you. The devil, I promise it. You can stay fifty yards away if you like."

"Walk by yourself," she said, but as he was pulling his staff from the eaves he had felt with his hand and found the bothy door open.

He pulled it shut. Put his back to it. "What did you see?"

"Nothing. I didn't look."

"Why shouldn't you look?"

"Because—"

She stopped. He could not see the shame in her face. She turned her head away and said, "Because I wouldn't like you to go staring at me or *my* things, unless I said you could."

He stood for a moment. Then he said, "Well, come on. If you want." He set off down the path to the creek, tapping the stones.

She followed him at fifty yards. She stepped very quietly. She was not sure she wanted him to know she had come.

Raím walked along the northern edge of the Tells, among the rich old middens. He followed the path downward to where the creek, swollen with spring melt, nearly swamped the stepping-stones. Using his stick for balance, he crossed with hardly a pause.

Because her legs were short Kat had to leap from rock to rock. When she climbed the far bank Raím's straight back was disappearing into the junipers. She followed him up the path and into the clearing below the Blessing Tree.

Buds studded the twigs, but the cast shadows were still branchy and bare. In their crisscross Raím knelt, dipped his hand into the pool, and put his wet palm over one eye, then the other. He rose, cocking his head as though he listened.

Kat stood still. There was no sound but magpies, the whisper of grass. Raím set off on the path toward Dark Heart slowly, as if burdened.

She hurried after him. At the pool's edge she thought of the ivory seal in its honeycomb and stumbled; her foot sent a shower of gravel tinkling down into the watercress.

Raím turned his head. He did not speak, but walked on more lightly.

After that Kat was too proud to be silent. She whistled and kicked stones. The path bent and followed the mountain flank. Raím's stick seemed to know every bush and boulder on the trail.

Kat cleared her throat. "Do you walk all the paths in the hills?"

"Just this one."

"Why?"

He would not answer.

To the left were stands of maples and cypress and aspen; to the right Dark Heart rose, covered with thorns. There had been a burn there once, and now the mountainside was thatched and interwoven with blackberry and barberry, hawthorn and scrub oak, dense as a dog's coat. Only the smooth track they were walking pierced the thicket.

"Where are we?" said Kat.

"On the hunters' path, to get past Dark Heart."

"We're *on* Dark Heart. I thought we weren't supposed to be."

"This is the Mother's lap, this brambled slope.

She lets us pass on this path only. No one goes on the rest of her anymore—not even women. This path leads to the wilderness where she lets men hunt."

"Where are we going?"

"On a walk."

"What if we meet hunters?"

"They're all at the Holds, readying their gear. There's a Long Hunt going out in two days."

"Tell me where we're going!"

"You don't have to come."

She followed him, frowning. When the path bent right to start up the canyon she said, "It would have been shorter to cut through the brambles."

"Try it!"

She practiced Jekka's rude hand gesture at the small of his back.

Here there was still snow in the corries, and the scrawny oak was without sign of leaf. They climbed among fir and black pine, and Kat's breath left her. The world seemed to expand under her feet; the air was thin. She stared up into the blue lake of the sky, and then she looked down between the pines and saw Creek and the Tells, plain as anthills.

"Raím! The Tells! You can see the pattern of the old streets—look!"

"I can't look."

"I'm sorry."

"I remember how it looks."

They broke out of the pines. The world was wide, light, full of wind. They stood at the edge of gray cliffs, and the air was loud with rushing: pine wind, stone wind, the roar of water far below.

"Out of this gorge the creek flows." Raím had to raise his voice. "Its wellspring rises in a cave; everything comes out of the dark."

Wind cracked the hems of Kat's culottes.

"Everything returns to the dark," said Raím. "Sooner or later."

"Raím, step back. The edge is very near."

"I know where I am. Shall I tell you? To my left is the valley plain, red and green and yellow: Creek and the Tells. To my right are the Mother's shoulder and the path going on up the canyon. There's a boulder shaped like a hare. Across the canyon the mountain range goes north. In front of me is the chasm." He stepped forward. "Two steps ahead is the edge—then air."

"Don't!" Kat sat down hard on the dirt and grabbed a gnarled root to anchor herself.

"Don't what?" he taunted.

Crouching, she crawled back through the brambles to a twisted pine and clutched its trunk. "Get back from the edge! You're cursed; you *act* cursed. You can't see it, but I can!"

He said, "I see it all the time."

But he came away from the edge. She clung to the tree, ready to retreat farther.

Back from the rim, the wind quieted. Raím sat down on the hare-shaped boulder and said, "That night. When you ran into me. You'd looked down that hole on the Tells and you saw it."

"I saw nothing. Black. Nothing!"

"*You saw it.* Death. That's what frightened you. Be damned, you think you're the only one death calls to?" He waved his hand toward the cliff. "She calls to me here."

"I don't want to know about it!"

"I wanted to show you. This is where I—"

"I'm going back!"

"Wait. I have to tell you. The devil—I've never told anybody." Through his teeth, he said, "Please."

She crouched where she was, holding on to the pine.

He spoke in a rush. "We were hunting mountain goat. It was summer. We walked along singing, not

97

on the path but on the cliff's edge. Just for joy—
there was no danger; it's granite, granite is sound. I
walked first. I always walked first. In the chasm I
saw a hawk, hanging in the air. I thought, Oh, if
I could fly! I stepped—" He leaned forward. With
horrible difficulty he said, "You stupid girl. I'm
insane with it. I lie awake thinking of it. I swear this:
in the instant that I stepped, before my foot touched,
I knew the stone was bad. I don't know how I
knew it. *But I knew.* Knowing, I chose to step, and
stepped." He put his fists to his eyes. "And I flew."

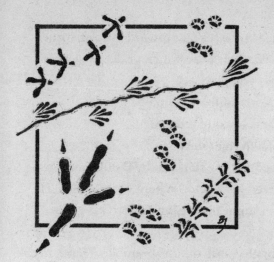

9

IN THE SILKY AIR beyond Raím's shoulders a turkey vulture drifted motionless. "I flew," he said. "Upside down I saw Dark Heart, and that was the last I saw."

"Why are you telling me this?" said Kat.

"Because in Creek you'll hear that I'm cursed, pitiful, the man whose dice fell wrong. But you have to know: *I chose this.* I don't understand it. But I chose."

She let go of the pine—not easily, for the bark glistened with pitch. "You come up here a lot."

"Yes. I come because I think it would be better to

finish it." He turned his face toward the cliff, turned back, and said, "But I can't. I can't do it, because I have to know why I chose."

"Come down off the mountain."

"I'm insane. I had to tell you."

"Come down right now."

He groped for his staff, said, "Damn!" and put his hand over his eyes. "Where's my stick?" He took a step, caught his toe, and fell to his knees. "I can't *see!*"

She struggled out of the brambles. "Take my hand."

"I'm not your child!"

"I'm not your mother. The stick's by your foot."

The turkey vulture wheeled and vanished. Raím put up his hand and said, "Please help me."

Kat said, "You were right about what I saw down that hole on the Tells." She took his hand in her pitchy one.

"The devil!" said Raím. "What's this sticky stuff?"

"Olive oil will take it off," said Kat.

"Don't have any," said Raím. He was hunched on the bench by the closed door of the bothy, clasping and unclasping his sticky hand.

"Rub it in dirt, then."

Once off the mountain Kat had dropped Raím's hand, or perhaps he had pulled it away. They had walked along unspeaking. When they came to the bothy he had lumped down on the bench without a word.

Kat knelt and scrubbed her palms in the cool windrows of dust against the bothy wall. "Come on. This dirt's so fine it's almost clay. You'll hardly feel it." She dusted her hands on her pinafore. "I'd bring you oil, but I don't know if I'll come again."

"Because I'm insane?"

"Because you're obnoxious."

A blue-tailed lizard scuttled around the corner of the house, with Brook pouncing after it. The fine silt recorded the chase: the lizard's track ended behind the rain barrel; Brook's footprints blotted out the lizard's and ended under Brook. He sniffed the shadows.

Kat picked him up and squeezed him until he made a little squeak like the last note from a bagpipe. The cat-and-lizard track reminded her of the potsherd in her pocket. She pulled it out and nudged it at Raím's unsticky hand. "Feel this."

"A broken mug." A reluctant smile curled the

corner of his mouth. "Here's a deer-mouse track. By damn—deer mice! I'd forgotten about them. Where'd you get this?"

"On the Tells."

"I don't notice anything unless it barks my shins. Creek pottery isn't like this. I like this."

"You don't like Creek pottery?"

"It's boring. All smooth. Except the common rough stuff that's for cooking—I like that."

"I thought so! At the potting shed I was pinching the coil and I thought about you, that you'd like to feel the fingerprints in the clay."

"You'd talk to me about potting? That's women's private stuff," said Raím with distaste. Then, "You thought about me?"

"I guess I shouldn't."

She did not say which question she was answering. Raím would not ask. This made him angry, and he shouted, "Creek makes everything smooth and nice. No rough edges, no crazies. By the holy, I go to that place as little as I can."

"You came to my bear, though."

"I felt like it. I'm initiated; they can't stop me."

"Why should they?"

"You think they should. You think, Raím's a pitiful half-man."

"I do not! How would you know what I think?"

"I can guess."

"You," said Kat, "are a bad guesser. You're a bad listener, too, which is why you don't know what I think. Give me back my deer mouse."

He held out the potsherd with sarcastic courtesy. Then he rubbed his eyes and said, "Oh, hell. Thanks for showing me."

"You're welcome," she said coldly. Then she relented. "Look. I don't mean *look*, but look, would you keep it for me? I'm not supposed to have it. I'm supposed to be learning to paint the Bear's Eye sign, and the Creek."

"I know those. I'm supposed to be weaving them."

"Supposed to be? Then—you don't?"

Instantly he was belligerent. "I'm blind! It's hard enough doing what I already know how to do. You think I'd muck around experimenting?"

"Bian says you're a fine weaver."

"Damn Bian. I *am* a fine weaver. Very fine, very boring. I do deathly ordinary stuff—stuff a blind man can handle."

She frowned at him. "I think you *do* muck around."

"The devil! Are you asking me to show you my loom?"

"Do you think I'd want to see it? It's just that when somebody as arrogant as you are gets humble, it's suspicious. Raím, *I'd* experiment, if I lived out here with nobody snooping on me. Imagine, not to have Mía watching me paint the Bear's Eye!"

"You *think* you'd experiment, you naive little cub."

She squeezed another squeak out of the cat, to remind him who it was Brook preferred to visit.

He beat his knees with his fists. "All right! So I experiment. Damn it, you're a woman, I shouldn't tell you anything. I experiment so bloody little you'd think I was a garden spider, always weaving the same web, yet you should see how nervous it makes them at the Holds. And I'll do more—I *will* do more. I don't have any damn thing to lose."

Kat put Brook down so he could visit Raím's ankles, but Raím stood up restlessly. "This world's small, it's dark," he said. "I don't want to weave the same cloth forever. This whole pattern—if I could let it go!"

"You can't live without patterns. It would be like having no bones."

"I just want to change them. There must be a place where you can change them. The place all patterns came from, before the world was made." He put his hand over his eyes and said, "I could fly to it. I know I could. I could *see* a new pattern, and bring it back to my loom."

"I knew a man once. He could go to that place. Only it was songs he heard there, and brought back."

"Was he your lover? He was. It's in your voice."

"That's none of your business."

"Some Leagueman laddie."

"He was not!"

"You're right—not if he sang. Leaguemen never sing unless they're drunk. Did your father get drunk and sing?"

"You leave my father alone!"

"I thought you hated him. They said you ran away."

"He's *my* father! You don't know him."

"I know about Leaguemen. I've seen them in Ten Orchards, getting drunk. I've traded with them for mirrors and perfume to give to girls—well, I didn't trade with the Leaguemen themselves. I got the stuff from the shopkeeper, but he got it from the Leaguemen. Everything was twice the price I'd pay if they were still allowed to trade in Creek."

"You hypocrites! You hate the Leaguemen, but you want your perfume. You just push them one step out of sight."

"Exactly. We sweep them under the rug. I've woven a rug or two. Creek likes its universe to be clean—or to *look* clean, at least."

"You're part of Creek!"

"My dear," he said, "so are you."

Defeated, Kat said, "The world's a bad place!"

"Yes, it is. What can you do about it? Shut your eyes to it, like Bian? The hell—at least I *know* I'm blind."

"I love Bian."

"You love your father," said Raím. "You defend him. And Bian wants to make him disappear."

"I don't love my father," she said, but very low.

"You love a singer. Maybe. It's true the world's bad. But it's good that you brought me off Dark Heart." Raím shook himself like a dog. "I'm done with my anger. It's like meat, I must have it. Go away now. I'll ask Set for olive oil."

He felt with his dirty hand, found a chink in the wall beside the bothy's closed door, and laid the potsherd there. "But you'll have to come back. Sometime. If you want to look at your deer-mouse track. Go paint the Bear's Eye, and I—I will weave."

She said, "Is it so terrible, all the time?"

"All the time."

🐢 🐢 🐢

ALEE, ALEE, my little spotted goat *ala*.
Alee, alee, my nimble yellow goat *ala*.

Kat sang softly. Flat on her stomach among the juniper and dry grass a little north of the Tells, she was poking an anthill with a straw.

She had found two tiny blue glass beads that the ants had brought up, and had threaded them on a piece of grass. They were the color of Raím's eyes. The sandy stillness was creased only by the wind. The backs of Kat's legs were sunburned, her hands were sticky, and Zella's wicked goat was nibbling her heels.

"Stinking goat," she said.

The billy reeked. A little while ago Kat had found him among the sagebrush where he should not have been and had bribed him with corn bread from her sash pouch. Then she had stuffed the pouch into the pocket of her pinafore and tied the green sash to his collar. He had come along with her, resentful but docile, eyeing the leather pouch.

The afternoon was done. Blue shadows poured across the valley. After she left Raím's bothy Kat had dawdled the whole day under the spacious sky, stopping to look at deer mouse highways that were pecked with footprints, although no mouse was to be seen. The grassland was waking with spring; there were snake trails, fox tracks, the dimpled roadways of the darkling beetle. The billy's cloven hoof made a mark like a broken heart.

I could draw all those tracks in clay, she thought. Everything leaves a track. Everything I touch, I mark; everything marks me.

The turbulence of the morning drained away, leaving solitude and peace. She allowed herself to think of Nall—the light touch of his lips on her mouth. She thought, I've still got that. Nobody can take that away.

The billy put his foot into the anthill. The frantic ants reminded Kat of Creek's bustle and she got up, saying, "It's late."

Flapping the sash, she cried, "*Alee, alee!*" and set out toward the creek path at a trot.

Hearth smoke rose over the town in blue banners. Kat thought of supper. So did Zella's goat. He lipped the pouch in her pocket, circling her until she had to turn around to unwind herself from the sash.

"No you don't, you bad goat," she said.

A voice hissed, "Tsst!"

She stopped. Looked around. Saw only juniper and nodding grass. The hair prickled on the back of her neck.

"Hey!"

She looked up into a tree and saw Raím, vivid among the green branches.

He was laughing, his eyes full of light. For a crazy instant she thought that by magic the world was made well, all curses healed. Her hand flew to her breasts.

Raím said, "Aren't you a darling!" and turned into Set, slithering down with a snapping of twigs, his spindle and cudgel at his waist. His bare legs shone with sweat and he reeked, like the goat.

"I saw you coming. I mean I saw you coming and going and winding and unwinding, like

109

Leaguemen fighting over a length of cloth. I hid, but you wouldn't have noticed if I'd lain down in front of you. Where'd you steal that ugly beast?"

He talked so fast. Kat said with a gasp, "I thought you were Raím, up in a tree!"

"Raím! Raím can't fly. I can." In one motion Set was back on the branch. "I hang around with the magpies and spy on the prettiest girl in Creek. But she smells like a goat."

"I do not!"

"Who said you were the prettiest girl in Creek?" She scowled.

"You are, though. Where've you been?"

"Out." The goat wound himself around the tree. Kat prayed for Set to climb down and go away. He smiled and swung his feet. Unwinding the goat, she said, "Why did you hide? If you wanted to talk to somebody, you could just ask."

"It's more fun this way, little somebody. You jumped two feet. Besides, everybody's after me. My brother—I've just come from his place—he's weaving like the fiend's in him, yelling at me to bring him this, bring him that. I've got my own life." He leaned his chin on his palm. "You know, your eyes change color, like the water in the creek."

110

"Why do you talk so much?"

"Men talk lots when they're courting."

She frowned up at him, pushing back her mop of hair.

He leaped down and caught her by the wrist.

"Let me go!" She tugged and flailed.

"Is this pitch, lassie?" He caught her other wrist and the sash, turning both her black palms to the sun. Half laughing, half angry, Set said, "Is that how he got pitch on his hand? He was shouting for olive oil. Were you holding hands with my brother?"

She jerked away. "You horrible boy! He fell down and lost his stick. I helped him back to the path. The pitch was on my hands." She stamped her foot. "Don't you care about him?"

Set shrugged, playing with the end of the sash. "Have you tried caring about Raím? I'd sooner pet a porcupine."

"He's your *brother*!"

"Don't I know it. Who hunts for Mister Manners, while he weaves things that will get him into worse trouble than he's already in? And he always took my girls, when he had his eyes." Set grinned. "He can't have you."

"I am not your girl!"

"I could arrange it. So you saved his neck? I bet old Raím loved *that*, having to ask a girl for help."

"You're cruel!"

"You're cruel to me. Look—I'll be gone on the Long Hunt, but when I come back the moon will be full and there'll be a dance. Come to it, darling, and dance with me."

"I'm not supposed to. Give me my goat."

"The grannies won't let you dance?" He grinned, and with the tassels on the sash he dusted her nose. "Listen, if you want me to bring you your bear, be nice to me!"

She snatched the sash from his hand and started toward Creek.

But Zella's wicked goat yanked the sash away; he nipped the pouch out of her pocket with his yellow teeth and bounced off across the sage.

"*Goat!*" cried Kat.

Laughing, Set gave chase. He ran like a jackrabbit, swift and dodging in the long gold light. Gaining on the billy, he caught the sash, and after a tussle for the pouch he ambled back, feeding the goat the last of the corn bread.

Panting, he put pouch and sash into her hand. "Here you are, love."

"I didn't ask for help!"

"You needed it. I'm a pest, aren't I? You'll get used to me. I'm just really rude, all the time."

It was uncanny to hear those words from him whose face was so like Raím's, and so unlike. Kat said, "Raím said that. About himself."

"He did? It's true." For an instant the teasing left Set's face and a shadow passed over it, anger or grief. "He brought it on himself. He was a man of men. He could have looked where he was stepping. He could have looked." Set rubbed his eyes, and the cocky mischief was back. "Raím's just rude. I'm rude, but I'm so sweet; aren't I sweet to you?"

"I hate it!"

"Fussy little woman! It's only courtship."

She was tongue-tied—furious and flattered and ashamed.

"You're so pretty," said Set. He shone with the energy of his run. "You talk with an accent, and your hair's short like a boy's. You're angry, and your eyes change, and you're a Leagueman's child." Taking hold of her curls, he leaned forward and kissed her open mouth.

She put her hand to her lips.

"Was that so bad?" he said.

She broke away from him and ran, the billy lolloping after her.

Set laughed, but did not follow. "Run home, cub," he said. "For a little while."

10

"HUSBAND!" cried Bian's impatient voice.

Emmot was smoking by the gate. As Kat came skidding around the corner she saw him glance over his shoulder at the house, where the voice came from. Then he settled down to his pipe, proving that he would not be ordered to dinner like a child.

Kat slapped open the gate. "I'm sorry I'm late! Zella's wicked goat—"

Emmot pulled his pipe from his mouth and grinned. "That's no worry of mine."

"Husband!"

"Seems like your aunt has worries," he said, replacing the pipe.

Jekka came out the door. "Eat it cold, then, Dad!" she shouted. "Oh—Kat!" She dodged as Mamik scrambled past her into the house, leaving a muddy handprint on her apron. "You dirty little turtle, go wash your hands. Kat, where were you? Mía said you went for clay; we looked for you by the creek. Mamik, did you hear me? Don't touch that. Dad!"

Kat put her hand to her mouth, where Set's kiss had rubbed out the trace of Nall's kisses, light and few, the way Brook's feet had rubbed out the lizard's track—the way this sociable chaos was smothering her solitude.

"What's the matter?" said Jekka. "Are you sick? This house is a hog market. Mother's in a fit. And where's the clay? Did you leave it at the shed?"

"Clay," said Kat, staring around as if she expected to see it.

"Come in or go out," cried Bian from the hearth. "Dolts in the doorway, all of you. Mamik, drop that! Cub, here's the whole world searching for you and you run off like some silly lass—where were you, kissing the boys behind a bush?"

Kat shouted, "I was not!"

She ran past the hearth to her bedroom and slammed the door. In the sudden silence they heard her sobbing, hard and desolate, over the whistling kettle.

"Oh, Mother," said Jekka.

"Ouma," said Bian, covering her eyes. "Ouma eat my sharp tongue." She took off her apron and gave it to Jekka. "Daughter, feed our men." Softly she opened the door to the bedroom and closed it after herself.

"Little bear," said Bian, "I'm sorry."

At the sound of her aunt's voice Kat's terrible crying choked itself to silence and she lay rigid, panting.

Bian sat down on the creaking straw mattress. "Kat, I was cross and cruel. Forgive me, daughter."

Kat said nothing.

"Mamik was being a trial, and Emmot was his dear, mulish self. It was wrong of me to take my anger out on you. But I was worried. Where were you? The girls looked, but you weren't where you said you'd be."

Kat turned her face slightly, away from Bian. "I found Zella's wicked goat."

"And he led you a chase? That billy! He's dashing

117

and disobedient, just like a man. You caught him and brought him back to Zella?"

"Yes."

"And I scold you for the good you do. I'm a bad old woman." Bian laid her hand on Kat's tense back. "I had no right to think it was the boys. You're my good girl."

Kat dragged up her hand as if to wipe her nose. She touched her mouth instead. In a flat, hard voice she said, "My father told me I'm a slut."

"See what dirt I've stirred up from the pond bottom. Your father! You know what I think of your father."

Kat turned over. "You can't make him disappear."

"Would that I could, and have my sister back."

"But you can't! He's *here*. The Leaguemen are here—on all the highways of the world, outside of Creek."

"Then let the world outside devour itself. That's not our concern. There were no Leaguemen in the world that Ouma made; therefore there are no Leaguemen in the real world that I choose to live in."

"The world was real before," said Kat. "When I lived by the sea. There were Leaguemen in it and it was real."

"I'm sure it seemed real," said Bian, "but it wasn't the true world. You know I go to the sea myself, sometimes; I sell pots and cloth and I dance the Long Night dance. And every time I come home more thankful that I live here in the true center of the universe, on Ouma's knees. You, little bear"— she touched Kat's arm—"you might have gone there with the pot-sellers at the winter solstice. Why didn't you want to? I remember there was a lad you loved a little. You might have seen him."

Kat turned on her face and spoke into the bed-clothes. "I wanted to wait until I'd gone to my bear."

"That was properly felt." Bian sighed. "Oh, my child. Love is easy. It's living that's hard."

"I know."

"No, you don't know. Not until we bring you another bear."

"I don't want another bear."

"I should think not, after what happened. But you will."

"I won't. Bian, I'm not like the girls here!"

"Yes, you are."

"I'm not. I never played in the creek when I was little. I never danced. I never watched my father weave."

119

"Of what use would that be, to watch a man weave!" Bian laughed.

"He might be wondering about things. He might be trying to find new patterns, or feeling how . . . how to keep living in the world. Like me," said Kat, desperate to be understood. "He might be trying to be happy."

"My goodness! Men have their own thoughts, and good luck to you if you think you understand them. Their great looms, of course, are none of our business, but you can watch Emmot at his hearth loom. Heaven knows I have, for twenty years. Emmot's happy. For all the gray in his hair he's just the merry lad I loved first."

Bian nudged Kat, as Jekka might. "He's calmer, though. Once when he and I were courting he smuggled a dozen chickens into our privy. It was dark there and the chickens went to sleep, until in the middle of the night my granny went out in her nightie and started to sit down." She chuckled. "Those were good times. It's true you've missed a lot of learning. But all the more do you need the bear."

She drew up her feet like a girl and sat cross-legged on the bed. "Look, my cub! The world is full of things, all rushing about: stars, winds, lovers, the changing seasons. The signs and rites give shape to it. Without them the day would fall in on itself.

"Ouma is the center. She eats you; then you are a woman, safe in the center of the world. Look north, to the star the whole world turns on—that's the Navel Star, the navel of the bear."

"In my old land we called it the Axle Star."

"There were navels before axles."

Kat took hold of Bian's wrist. "But what ate Ouma to make her a woman?"

Bian's silence was long. When she spoke her voice was troubled. "Who have you been talking to, to put those ideas in your head?"

"Nobody! You think I can't have ideas of my own!"

"Those thoughts are bad. They're craziness."

"They're not! I only wondered—if you lift up the rug, what's under it?"

"The rug? There is no rug. Ouma is what the world is made of—its very clay. Can you lift up the earth? Look behind the stars? Dear cub, can you?"

"No."

"Then why do you try?"

"Maybe *they* were trying to look behind the stars—those women who lived in the Tells. When they went up Dark Heart without knowing what might eat them."

"Those women are bones now, and the Tells are rubble."

"But were those women never eaten by anything good? Sometimes did they find *new* signs, *new* rites, and bring them back to the loom—I mean, to the Clay Court?"

"Maybe they did," said Bian. "Sometimes. But how often? And at what risk? The great, the saints— they are the ones who have holy visions. Not little people like you and me. And even for them the price is high, in years and tears and loneliness. Kat, is that what you want? To be called farther and farther from your home, into the wilderness?"

"No . . ."

"Of course not. Your mother chose to leave us, and died of sorrow. Don't tell me otherwise—it was sorrow! Now her daughter wants what Lisei never had: a good husband, babies, evening laughter, her place in the Circle. Isn't that so?"

"Yes." It was true. Kat laid her hand over her eyes.

"Bear cub. You've had a hard start on the path. You are so near the goal; don't falter now. Keep walking, my daughter." Bian's voice was trustworthy, sure. "One day you will see how confusing the world is without Ouma, and you will ask for her yourself. You'll ask for your bear. Then you'll see the world as a woman, and I promise you that everything will look different."

She stroked Kat's snarled red curls. "I loved your mother. I braided her hair the night she left us, not knowing I would never see her again. I love her daughter always—now, while she is a cub, and later, when at last she will go to her bear."

Kat dropped her hand and lay looking up, her face blotched and still.

Smiling, Bian patted her thigh. "Wash your face, little one. Be happy."

Kat strung the two blue beads on a thread and hung them around her neck against the bear scars. While she delayed, unwilling to meet the family's eyes, the bedroom had grown dark. She was starving. She splashed her face at the washbowl and opened the door to the smell of rabbit stew.

Bian and Jekka were gone, but Emmot was there, tethered to the hearth by his sash loom. Mamik leaned sleepily on his father's thigh; the chirp of his incessant questions ran slower and slower, like a cricket in cool weather.

"Feel better?" said Emmot in his cautious voice.

"I'm all right."

Emmot nodded. He continued to weave, in silence.

Under his fingers a bright red butterfly of coiled yarn flew from one side of the growing sash to the other. Sometimes it paused, and a black butterfly or a white one flew instead, leaving the sinuous curve of the Creek sign behind it. The batten tapped the pattern into place.

Kat dipped up a bowl of stew. Mamik had stopped his questions and hid behind his father.

There was no sound except the flutter of the fire, the thump of the batten. Kat felt suddenly as though eating were a very slushy, public act. She finished the stew and set the empty bowl on the hearth with a sigh.

Mamik peered at her over Emmot's knee. Kat thought Set must have had curls like that when he was little; Raím too. Mamik blinked like an owlet.

"Mamikimi," she said to him, "would you like some peppermint tea?"

He slid down out of sight. But his voice said, "I want honey in it."

"I'll bring the honey pot. Uncle, would you like some too?"

Emmot said, "I would, thank you," then sank back into silence as Kat swung the kettle over the fire.

She glanced at her uncle as they waited for the water to boil. It was impossible to imagine Emmot young and impudent like Set, or with a bitter and desolate face like Raím's. Emmot and his loom were changeless, as much a part of the hearth as the broom.

She handed him his steaming mug, and a smaller one, with the honey pot, for Mamik, who was still in hiding.

"Uncle," she said, "will you go on the Long Hunt?"

Emmot shook his head. "I'm not so young as I was. Got better things to do."

He was looking at the hearth loom, but absently. Kat wondered whether he was seeing another loom; one neither she nor Bian had ever seen.

"Uncle," she said, "how old were you when you learned to weave?"

He swiveled in the loom harness and stared at her. "Pretty young. A boy."

"Mamik's learning, isn't he? He asks so many questions."

"He'll make a weaver." Emmot rescued the honey pot from Mamik and leaned to set it on the hearth, slackening the tension on the loom. The Creek sign rippled in the firelight like a snake. Kat remembered that Emmot, too, must have a snake tattoo around his hips.

"That's beautiful," she said, of the sash.

Emmot sucked his tea. "It'll do."

Kat looked at the plane of threads that stretched up like a harp to be played. Pointing, she said, "What do you call that?"

"The warp."

Mamik popped up like a woodchuck. "I can spin yarn for the warp. I'm good."

"Hush," said Emmot, but he smiled and stroked the sash as though he loved it.

Kat said, "Uncle, show me how the loom works."

"Well." Emmot shifted his feet. "That's for boys."

"I know."

"Girls don't ask. But then, if they're born here they see the hearth loom every day. When they see their dad."

"I didn't see my father much," said Kat. "He was away."

"Nor could he weave. That's hard on a man."

Emmot scratched his head. "And it's hard on you, starting so late. I'll show you a little bit, so you know. That wouldn't do any harm, would it?"

Kat wanted to say, "I love you, and I'm glad you're my uncle." But she had never said anything like that, so instead she said, "Oh, please show me!" and touched the heddle rod.

"You're a good lass," said Emmot. Then before Kat could respond he frowned and said, "Listen, then. This is the warp beam. Here he's just a stick, but still we call him the great beam, or . . . Well, you're not a boy. There are names you shouldn't know. But you can say 'the great beam.' It was by the great beam that Ouma caught her husband."

"Ouma's husband was named Trouble," Mamik said sleepily.

Kat said, "Bian told me that."

Emmot grinned. "She would! But do you know the tale? Ouma's lonely; she asks for a man and he comes—that's Trouble. Ouma sets a brass ring in her hearth and she ties Trouble's loom to it, here at the great beam."

"That's so he can't leave her," said Mamik.

"But Trouble fools her. With his cudgel haft he

pries open the ring and makes it a hook, like that one where my loom's tied. He unhooks his loom, and off to the wilderness he goes."

"But he comes back." Mamik yawned and sighed. "Ouma makes rabbit pies."

"A man does get hungry. Still, from that day to this, Trouble keeps his great loom outside the town walls, in the Loom Holds. On the hearth loom he weaves trinkets like this sash—nothing of importance. East to west he weaves, with the sun, but in the Holds—" Emmot stopped, his brow puckered. "Well, I can't tell you that. But look here, this is the cloth beam. It hitches to my sash. These are heddles."

Kat said, "And in your hand, that's the batten. You beat the yarn into place with it."

"We say it sets the whole world in order. The cudgel, we call it."

"The cudgel," said Kat. "Like for the bear?"

"Yes. Well. The same name."

He would not look at her, but tapped his fingers on his thigh. He nodded at Mamik and said, "See that son of mine! Gone fast asleep."

"Uncle, who brought my bear?"

Emmot pulled at his mustache. "We all did. We're men. But it was the young men who caught her; they must." With angry apology he said, "She was little but fierce. You've got no reason to be ashamed. The hunter who brought her from her den she marked from hip to knee."

"Who was that?"

"Set."

Emmot bent over Mamik. When he raised his head his face looked young and open. "Don't grieve for what's happened. You're still a lovely lass." Then he scowled. "Get along now. I've told you more than I've told my own daughter."

Kat stared into her empty mug.

He said, "Don't ask about the loom. There's a bit of time coming to you now, with the boys at the hunt and the streets quiet. Use it to study what you've missed. And that's not the loom.

"Be one with us here in Creek. Paint pots, court lads, dance, go to your bear. There's happiness in it." He unfastened the loom from his sash and hung it on the brass hook. As he swung the sleeping Mamik over his shoulder he said, "Don't act different. You have a hard enough time ahead of you as it is."

11

"SMELL THE FLOWERING olives," said Kat.

"You must have a nose like a wild dog," Jekka panted. "All I can smell is goat dung."

They were trudging along the south wall of town with carry cloths full of dry manure on their backs. The morning was warm and still, almost summery—just right for firing pots.

The Long Hunt was over. For three weeks the streets of Creek had been empty of young men, and Kat had had a respite from Set's whistles and grins. Then last night the hunters had come home.

There had been a fire at the Hearthstone. The young men dumped down their packsacks full of half-smoked jerky and unslung from poles the fresh carcasses of deer. They had killed antelope, and an elk. They were full of stories of their exploits, which got better and better as the night went on.

This morning they lounged on the street corners, in need of an audience. Kat and Jekka had been jostled and teased all the way to the goat pens. They did not run into Set until they had filled their carry cloths with the stinking dung and were plodding toward the Clay Court. He said nothing to them, but clutched his nose, staggered, and fell dead.

Kat thought she would wither up with shame. Seeing Set made her think of Raím as well, and feel guilty, for she had not gone back to visit him again.

She told herself it was because every instant of the last three weeks had been occupied by some lesson crucial to her initiation. Someone was always teaching her, and she could never sneak away. But in fact she had seen Raím twice: once behind the granaries and once, unaccountably, by her own front gate. She had not spoken to him. She did not want to upset Bian, and besides it felt eerie to see him in town, like seeing a stag in the marketplace.

Raím wouldn't be interested in what I've been doing anyway, she thought. He doesn't like Creek pottery.

And the pot that she would be firing today was perfectly Creek—smooth as an apple, a beautiful two-handled water jar painted with the Bear's Eye sign.

"That's good," Mía had said one afternoon last week, looking over Kat's shoulder.

Kat had jumped, nearly dropping Bian's grinding stone. After weeks of making and painting water jars she was so bored that she had to keep up a kind of running daydream in which, as her hands worked, her imagination roamed the hills like Zella's goat.

She had looked at her jar. It looked like every other jar—maybe that was why Mía had praised it. Kat said, "It's good?"

"You can fire that one. Can't she, Sisira?"

Sisira had frowned at the jar and its maker, in case Kat might think too much of herself. "I think she might. Do you begin to understand, cub, that beauty comes from doing what is right?"

Kat nodded. The other girls in the shed smiled with approval; it was they who had coached her all these weeks. Esangi, of course, had not even looked up. She was painting an enormous grain jar, the only one so far to survive its building, drying, and polishing; if all went well it would go into the next firing. That event would be much more notable than a cub's pinching out her first water jar.

"Put it on the drying shelves," said Sisira to Kat, adding, "and if Ouma is pleased with it maybe it won't explode in the kiln. But I advise you to assume that it *will* explode. Continue to work humbly."

"That pompous old stick," said Jekka when Sisira had gone. "Good for you, Kat!"

Kat had smiled, feeling happy. Back at her bench she had taken the next lump of clay from the bucket and slapped it down on the board between her knees.

It seemed too bad that it was bound to be another water jar. She almost envied Esangi; the grain jars looked interesting to build, even though most of them collapsed.

She set her palm on the lump and leaned hard, making a clear handprint. She picked it up and squeezed it. Coils of clay oozed between her fingers like snakes' heads.

"Rain snakes," she said aloud. The clay smelled like wet spring earth.

"Don't fool around," said Jekka. "You're doing fine, don't spoil it. It's only a week till firing day."

Kat had sighed, mashed the snakes together, and begun another water jar.

Now it *was* firing day. The teasing young men followed the girls to the Clay Court but could not enter. Once inside, Kat and Jekka dumped their carry cloths onto the dung pile by the main shed. A fire had been built in the open the night before, to dry the earth and bless it. Sisira was raking the coals. Benches had been set up to hold the raw pottery until the kiln was built.

Mía came out of the shed with an unfired bowl held carefully in both hands. "You're tortoises," she said to Kat and Jekka. "We brought fuel hours ago."

Jekka shrugged her lightened shoulders. "You know what it's like out there with the great hunters. We took the long way round. And Zella was at the goat pens; she wanted to talk about her wicked billy. She thinks Kat has bewitched him—but it's a nice curse, he hasn't run away in a month."

"It's corn bread," said Kat. "I bring him corn bread in the afternoons."

She wished Zella's billy *would* run away. Then she could go look for him instead of making water jars. She might even visit Raím. She wondered how Raím had managed with Set gone.

"Anybody could bewitch me with corn bread," said Mía. "I've been working since dawn." She set the bowl on one of the benches. "Go get your jar, cub. I'll make sure Sisira gives it a good place in the kiln."

"Thanks," Kat said shyly.

"It deserves a good place," said Mía. "It's perfect. You've worked hard."

After the daylight, the shed was dark as a pocket. Kat banged her knee on somebody's bench, but she did not care. She was so warmed by Mía's praise that as she lifted her jar from the shelves she sang her mother's lullaby:

> Bear in the black rock,
> Bear's two children.
> My red cub, O!
> My brown cub, O!

"Shut up that baby song. On firing day you have to sing firing songs."

It was Esangi.

She stood in the shadows next to the drying shelves. In her arms she carried her great grain jar, ready for the kiln. It was the first time she had spoken to Kat since the day she had threatened to smash the deer-mouse pot; it was the first time she had gotten Kat alone. "But I guess babies can sing baby songs anytime."

The words hung in the air like bait.

Sisira was not in the potting shed.

Kat saw it in her mind's eye as if it were already over: fists and legs tangled among the broken benches, her perfect water jar smashed before it was even brought to the kiln.

Then she realized, in the same flash, that Esangi was as vulnerable as she was.

With one clumsy tackle Kat could bring her down. The great jar that was to prove Esangi's skill would be dust—no matter what happened afterward. Even if Esangi beat her to a smear.

It was a fair trade for months of hatred. Kat set down her jar.

Esangi's eyes widened. As though she could escape she trudged slowly toward the door. The jar was enormous; she could barely carry it.

Daylight fell upon it.

It had a swelling belly like a pregnant woman's. Esangi had painted on it the signs for Creek and

Trout—the same old signs, but her brush had acknowledged the volume of the jar, the curve of its shoulder. Trout swam over it like minnows in shallows. After firing the fish would be green on lighter green.

It was beautiful. Not perfect—just beautiful, as if it were alive. Kat looked at her own jar. It was tight, correct, and as boring as its maker had been bored.

Her heart sank.

The moment passed; she did not jump, and Esangi made it to the door.

There she realized the tackle was not going to happen. Turning back, she said, "Coward!"

"No—it's that your jar's so lovely."

Esangi's jaw dropped. "You little toady!" she said. "Kiss somebody else's behind!" She lumbered out of the shed, toward the fire.

Shaken, Kat carried her jar into the sunshine. She looked at it again. "It's fine," she whispered. "It looks how it's supposed to look."

She set it on the bench with the rest of the younger girls' work. Beyond it she saw Esangi's jar again, its living shape.

"Trot, tortoise," said Mía. "There's more to carry."

Kat joined the crowd of girls who were hauling

rocks to the kiln site. Esangi ignored her. Kat thought, It's *their* fault my jar's boring. They wouldn't let me do anything else.

Together the women built a stone grate over the coals, knocking away cobbles that the heat had cracked too small. They set the month's potting mouth-down on the grate.

Chipped black saggers went over the finer pots to keep them from the smoke, while the kitchenware was left to smirch. Kat busied herself with this rough pottery. She did not want to look at her flawless, boring jar.

Cedar bark and juniper were piled over the pots. Sisira rejected this log or that, fussing and adjusting. The goat dung, good and dry, went over all. Goat was the best, Sisira announced loudly as she announced every firing day—better than mule dung, better than wood.

"Ouma bless Zella's wicked goat," Mía said piously, and snickered. With singing, the fire was lit. A reeking column of smoke rose up and smudged the blue sky.

The good weather held. They did not need the brush windbreak they had built. The air above the kiln rippled with heat like a mirage, and the breeze almost slept, though now and then a chance sigh puffed ashes and acrid smoke over the fire-tenders, filling their noses and hair.

"Phew!" Jekka wiped her stinging eyes. "It smelled better when we were carrying it. Oh!"

A muffled pop shook the firing stack. A pot had exploded. They could not tell which or where for the smoke. *Bang!* Another went, and a third.

"Three," said Jekka. "Not bad. It's the cubs' pots that blow up; they're a menace." She ran to toss another shovelful of dung on the pile.

By the time the fire had sunk everyone stank. It was late afternoon. Mothers sat on the benches and nursed their babies; Kat thought perhaps fewer women were keeping their infants' faces turned away from her. Bigger children poked the coals with sticks and were scolded. Even some boys who were really too old to be in the Clay Court wandered in, tossing their spindles, and were sent off with threats.

The pile had to cool slowly, so that the pots would not crack. Sisira circled it, prodding with a pitchfork and muttering, "Not yet."

"I can't wait to see your jar," said Jekka. "It'll be hot as andirons. Don't pick it up."

"I won't," said Kat.

What she meant was, I won't have to. Because she knew whose pot had exploded in the kiln.

She was both grateful and in despair. She would not have to feel confused about that perfect, boring jar anymore; on the other hand, she was doomed to keep making water jars until she could produce something that survived the fire.

> Clay makes us,
> Fire transforms us.
> Rise! Be at your work.

> Earth makes us,
> Love transforms us.
> Rise! Be at your work.

Chanting, Sisira parted the ashes with the tines of her pitchfork. A few younger women started to lift the smoky kitchenware on the ends of poles, setting the pieces on the sand pile that had been prepared for them. Carefully, with sticks and shovels, they raised the saggers, exposing the glossy painted pots.

The breeze blew; ashes flew in the air, flew in Kat's face. When her eyes stopped weeping she saw her perfect jar clean among the clinkers, shining as if newborn.

"There!" said Mía. "That's what you'll take to gather water from the Blessing Tree, cub, when you go to your bear."

"No," said Kat.

She was not speaking about her own jar, but Esangi's. With four poles the huge sagger had been lifted away to show . . . nothing. Nothing but a pile of shards like the scatter on the Tells, green on lighter green. Bright as water, a trout's eye winked from the heap.

From the edge of the ash pile Esangi watched, unmoving.

"Oh, too bad!" said Mía.

Someone brought Esangi a pitchfork to stir among the shards. She shoved it aside. Catching Kat's eye, she went red, went white.

But she said only, "What are you all howling about? It was a stupid *jar*. It's not like somebody died." Snatching the pitchfork, she began to lift the other pots to the sand pile, fast and recklessly.

She thrust one tine through the handle of Kat's jar.

"Careful with that," said Mía.

Esangi shouted, "Am I so clumsy?" With exaggerated care she carried the jar to the sand pile and laid it down. "You can sell that to the Leaguemen."

She stabbed the pitchfork into the dirt and stalked off, breaking into a run out the south gate.

"Don't mind her," said Mía. "She's prickly because her jar blew up."

"Esangi was *born* prickly," said Jekka. "I don't know how her mother stood it for nine months."

They scattered the ashes, teasing Bo, whose bowl had exploded and glued itself all over Selem's plate. By the time all the pots were shifted and cooled Dark Heart was red with sunset and it was almost too chilly to wash, but the women and girls ran along the creek to the millpond, laughing.

A few young hunters lounged on the bank. At the sight of the crowd of women, among them their own mothers, they scrambled up and away, trying to look nonchalant.

"Out!" cried the women. "The pond's ours, run along." Among the willows they pulled off their blouses and folded their skirts over the fragrant olive boughs. "Get in!" they told one another. "You're black as crows!" "What's worse, stink or cold water?"

"I won't wash here," Kat said to Jekka.

She had not bathed with the rest since the bear, but had washed alone in the tub at Bian's hearth.

"Oh, come on." Jekka tossed her ashy blouse onto

a rock. The blue tattoos on her breasts shone as if they had risen from within her. "Nobody cares about those scars." But she did not protest as Kat edged off into the rushes and waded far along the shore.

Kat hid behind a sandstone ledge that jutted out of the water, bound to the bank only by tamarisk and beavers' trash. There she took off her stinking clothes. Naked except for the two blue beads, she knelt among schools of minnows that nibbled her knees. She looked at herself.

Set would loathe me, she thought. If he ever saw all of me.

A bushy crackle sounded at her elbow, and a branch slapped the water. She whirled around, covering her breasts and crouching down in the muddy pond, away from Set's blue eyes.

But it was Esangi, floundering back from the ledge among the swampy withies, toward the shore. The tamarisks had her well hobbled. Rubbing furiously at the shine of her tears, she said, "Why're you spying after me?"

"I wasn't!"

"You were. If you weren't you'd be with the rest of them, getting drooled over for your baby jar." Esangi made a jerky motion toward Kat, as though to grab her and hit. "I made a jar like that when I was ten!"

Shuddering under cold water and Esangi's hatred, Kat said, "Mine's a bad jar."

"You groveling mutt! Say that again."

"It's a bad jar! You think I can't tell? It was the best I could do and it's stupid. What do you want me to say—that I was made bad, like the jar?"

"Yes! Say that."

"I *will*," said Kat. It was a relief to speak the truth, in grief and rage. "I *was* made bad. Mother and Father—I know they never liked my making. If they'd liked it I wouldn't be a hideous freak, and I'd be happy."

"Your father? Oh, I'm sure your *father* liked your making!"

"He didn't like anything. Not even his children. He was hardly ever home." Kat thought how absence could wound like a claw, except that the scars did not show. She stood up out of the water, dropping her hands from her breasts. "I wasn't spying. I came here to hide."

Esangi flinched. She said, "Be ashamed of your *father*, you stupid cub!"

"I said I was."

"You're ashamed of *yourself*! You cringe and creep as if you weren't female. It's your *father's* fault about the scars. If he hadn't raped your mother you'd have been born one of us, and we could love you."

Kat was so astonished that it was a moment before she could speak. "He didn't rape her. She chose to go with him."

"Of course he raped her! He was a Leagueman! He was a man, men ruin it, Leaguemen ruin it. They rape the women and ruin their daughters." Esangi had begun to cry, horribly, as though the crying did not want to come out of her. "You cringing pup! Will you be ashamed all your life because your mother was defiled by some dog of a Leagueman?" She could hardly speak. "Hate *him*! When you're a bear of the Circle you'll *have* to be proud."

Kat stood with her mouth open. A thought struck her like a snake. "Who was it who was raped on the road to Ten Orchards?" she said. "Was it your mother? Esangi, was *your* father a Leagueman?"

"I have no father! I was born to a woman, you dirty cub, and I wanted to be eaten by Ouma from the day I was born!"

But Kat was searching Esangi's face, which was wrenched with weeping.

Maybe it was a South Road Leagueman, she thought. Oh, god, I hope it wasn't one of my uncles. And it couldn't have been . . .

She wanted to vomit. It couldn't have been her own father. Could it? Her father would never do that.

But then she thought, Things went bad early between Father and Lisei. He was always away on business. I've heard him talking to my uncles about Ten Orchards; the women there were pretty, he said, but stubborn, and it was a good place to buy cloth.

"Did they catch the man?" she said in a panic. "Who was it? Tell me! Did your mother recognize him?"

"You shut up about my mother!"

Esangi began again to bash her way through the willow brush toward shore. Her braid caught on a snag and she fought with it, sobbing.

"Wait!" As if she could make some reparation, Kat floundered toward her. "You're caught, let me help you."

"Get away, you bitch!"

Kat stopped. Esangi struggled like a mouse with its leg in a trap. "Listen," said Kat. "Esangi, I'm sorry. I mean, it's your jar I'm sorry about. I wish, I *wish* it'd been mine that blew up!"

146

"I'm sure!"

"I do." Suddenly Kat was angry. "I don't care what you think. I don't care if you hate me. You do anyway. That was a wonderful jar!"

"I'll make another. I'm a potter. You're not, you're a fawning puppy. You lick Sisira's hand and say yes ma'am, no ma'am—"

"The devil I do!" Kat shouted, as if Raím's voice had borrowed her mouth. "You leave me alone! This cub has claws, sister; I'll scar you where a tattoo won't hide it!"

Esangi stopped struggling, as if she had been doused with cold water. She shook, locking up her last sobs, and the familiar mask of indifference came down over her face.

"Bitch. I'm running, I'm so scared." Returning to the safe world of insults, she said, "Keep it up, puppy. That's the first I've heard you bark."

"Puppies grow to be wild dogs."

"Wild dogs are dirt. They skulk among the Holds."

"They get meat there, and learn secrets."

"They get offal, and hunters' carrion—that's what you get from men." Esangi picked her braid from the branches. "Be careful, cub. You don't know anything. Listen! You're not a dog. You're a woman, be proud. I'll *make* you proud." She pointed her hard finger at Kat. "I'll teach you to make pots."

Kat stared. "Oh? You'll teach me how to paint the damned Bear's Eye!"

"Yes. You think Mía made you sweat? Just wait till you work for me."

"What makes you think I'll work for you?" Kat almost added, You think you can fix yourself by fixing me?

But she could not say it. Esangi's face was her own—tear-swollen, marked by events she had not asked for.

"You will," said Esangi. "Come to the potting shed tomorrow. Or do you want to go back onto the Tells and learn from ghosts?"

"Why not? I'm cursed already."

Esangi glared. "You're digging up spunk from somewhere. It must be from your mother." She turned and waded toward the shore.

Kat thought, I don't know if you're my half sister. But I know I'm not the one who's cursed.

Aloud she said, and meant it, "You take care."

"Mind your own business."

"What's my business?"

"Learning the signs and rites."

"I already know them," said Kat. "See?" She made Jekka's rude hand gesture.

Esangi gaped at her. Then she said, "Tomorrow, cub. In the potting shed."

12

NEXT MORNING everyone still smelled of goat-dung smoke, in spite of their swim. All the way to the Clay Court, Kat worried that she might meet Set and be teased, but she slipped through the red gate unseen.

The girls mixed the new clay, singing. Kat took a lump of it back to her bench and slapped it down.

Now that the fired pot had passed inspection, this clay would not have to become a water jar. Kat put the heel of her hand on the lump and leaned the whole weight of her body on it, feeling it move.

Suddenly Esangi was at her elbow, dragging up a second bench. "All right," she said. "We'll start."

"Start what?" said Jekka. "Esangi, what are you up to?"

"I'm teaching her." Esangi glowered around the room. "You were right and I was wrong. Sisira said to teach her, so I'm teaching her."

"What's got into you?" said Jekka. "Your pots should blow up more often."

"I'll blow your pot to where you can't find it, jaybird. I said I was wrong. Want to fight about it?"

Jekka shrugged. Yet Esangi had admitted her mistake. "Teach her the clay chant, if you're so eager. She forgets to say it."

Sisira looked pleased. "Teach her to grind paint. She never gets it fine enough."

"I'll teach her what she needs to know," said Esangi. She put her hard hands over Kat's on the lump of clay. "Here's how it's done, cub. Feel."

She leaned with her whole weight. The gesture, the clay, even Kat's hands became Esangi's.

"And you'll show her how you paint the Bear's Eye?" said Mía.

It was then that Kat had excused herself to the privy and let out Zella's goat.

It was easy. She left the potting shed by the back path, slipped through the little gate to the pens, and kicked two slats out of the fence. The billy was kept by himself because he was a troublemaker; Kat made sure he got his horns through the gap. Then all she had to do was go back to the potting shed and wait.

It worked. In less than an hour Zella came huffing to the shed, calling for Kat. "He likes you, dear," she said, in such a sweat with hurry and worry that she forgot to make the sign against cursing. "Go catch him, tcha! He'll be dogs' meat next, and deserve it!"

Dutiful, Kat left the potting shed. Once out of sight she ran so fast that one of her clogs split.

She took a back way to Bian's house. Nobody was there but Mamik and two other little boys, playing at weaving under the lilac bush.

"Go away!" they said. "You can't look!"

At the hearth, Kat put corn bread in her pouch. She poured olive oil from the crock into a jar that she corked with a broken corncob. Then, looking over her shoulder, she went into the bedroom, where she put her little finger into Jekka's perfume bottle and drew it along her collarbone.

It was terrific perfume, much stronger than lilacs. She dabbed a bit more on her wrists and felt better armored in case she should meet Set. She waited for a moment when the alley was empty, climbed out the bedroom window, and ran, clumsy on her broken clog.

Behind the pigsties she slowed down and strolled, sniffing herself.

Dark Heart was distant and blue. A group of barefoot children played with the old mare by the millpond. Kat watched them for a moment, then ducked down into the creek bed and headed upstream.

The walking was harder there, but she was less likely to be seen, and she might be looking for a goat among the reeds. Every now and then she called, "*Alee*, goat, goat."

The creek was brown and loud. She picked up round rocks and chucked them into the water.

North of the Tells she climbed out of the creek bed and struck off across the prairie toward the line of poplars. She was half-pleased, half-disappointed to see the unmistakable cloven tracks of Zella's goat headed in the same direction.

"I don't want to find him too fast," she said aloud.

"Of course, he's terribly, terribly hard to catch."

But when she got to Raím's dooryard, there was no sign of the billy but his dusty footprints and splashes that showed he had drunk from the rain barrel. The yard was empty. On the bench lay Raím's shaving kit: bucket, soap, kettle, and long razor.

The door was open. Feeling both rude and eager, she dropped her eyes.

"The devil!" howled Raím inside the bothy. "Son of all demons, imp's child, meddling shameless nameless nit!"

Kat looked up amazed as Brook, upside down, sailed spitting into a saltbush. Raím appeared in the doorway, panting with rage.

"Begone!" he shouted.

Brook gathered himself and dashed off in hare-like leaps, his tail fat as a teasel.

"Stop that!" said Kat. "Don't you hurt him!"

Raím froze. "You! *Where have you been?*"

"Who cares where I've been? What are you doing to Brook?"

"Damn Brook! Ah, damn you, too. Begone!"

"I won't. What have you done?"

"*I?* All devils!" Raím rubbed his eyes, ducked back into the bothy, and slammed the door.

Kat kicked the sand with the toe of her clog. She came close to the door and said, "I brought your rotten olive oil."

"Why the hell should I want it now!"

"In case you ever do."

"Damn you!" The door opened and Raím reappeared, blocking the opening with his body. "Pour it out. Drink it. Shove it you know where. Why didn't you come before?"

"I didn't feel like it. You might have killed Brook! You couldn't see where you were throwing him."

"I hope I killed him. Anyway, do you think I don't know my own front yard?" He sniffed. "What have you got on? You smell terrible."

"It's the firing smoke. Everybody smells of it."

"It's cheap perfume. You smell like Set when he's courting."

"I do not! It's Jekka's. I borrowed it because I smell like goat."

"You don't. You smell like girl. I like how you smell. Who said you smell like goat?"

"Set."

Raím's face clotted with fury. He stepped out, banging the door shut behind him.

"What are you doing, letting Set close enough to

know what you smell like? That oaf has a girl for every day of the week."

"That's just like you, from what I hear," said Kat.

Through his teeth Raím said, "It is."

As though he could see her he reached out and caught her blouse in his fist.

She could not move, could think only, Esangi, ruin, men.

He dropped his hand. "It *was*," he said.

He turned with a lurch. She had another flash of terror as he groped toward the open razor. But it was the kettle he took up, and drawing back his long arm he slashed it down across the bothy door.

Water flew, a white wound opened in the wood, the kettle dangled from its broken handle. Raím dropped it with a clatter and leaned his forehead on the door.

In a tight, polite voice he said, "You have not chosen a good time for your visit."

"You scared me!" she said when she could speak. She pressed her hands to her breasts, as she rarely did now that the claw wounds were healed.

"I scare myself. I told you I was insane. Set, Set! I was that manhood, those eyes. If you've come here to pity me I will kill you."

"I—I came to bring you olive oil."

"Out of pity. Why else?" He rubbed his eyes. "Why else?"

In a small, frightened voice she said, "I like you."

He turned around. There was a red mark on his forehead from the door, and she watched him blush until the red mark disappeared into his blushing. He said, "You do not."

She said nothing. Suddenly she was not sure she *did* like him.

He tried to sit down on the doorstep. He sat on the kettle. Cursing, he picked it up and seemed to stare at it; then he held it out. "Damn you! Would you like a cup of tea?"

"Tea—"

"Come inside. The stove's lit."

"You mean, I could come in there with the loom?"

"The devil," said Raím, sounding more like himself. "I suppose you can't."

"You could use the kettle to hammer up the curtain again."

"I need it for the tea."

"I'll sit on the step, then. Bring the tea out here."

"That's best." A peculiar look came over Raím's

157

face. He fidgeted, and opened his mouth as if to ask a question.

But he must have changed his mind, for he shook his head angrily, dipped the kettle in the rain barrel, went inside, and slammed the door.

Kat sat on the doorstep. She heard the clank of the kettle on the stove, a scuffling noise, a groan, and a curse.

Bees hummed.

She said to the door, "Did my goat come here?"

"*Your* goat! That foul hulk sucking my rain barrel! I kicked him and he ran off."

"Oh." Kat stared at the billy's footprints for a while. She asked the door, "What did Brook do?"

"Oh, god!"

"So, what did he do?"

"You wouldn't understand. It's about the loom."

"I know about looms."

"Like hell!"

"I do. I know about the heddles and the cudgel and the great beam."

Raím rattled the door handle. Kat scrambled off the doorstep and sat on the bench, averting her eyes. He came out and sat heavily on the step, his back against the door.

He said, "What you know about looms is nothing. Who taught you?"

"Emmot. Then he said not to ask him anymore."

"He wouldn't tell you." Raím stretched out his legs and sat in the sunshine, waiting for the kettle to boil. A meadowlark on a stone poured out its music.

At last he said, "In your old land, can a woman look on a man's loom?"

"Men there don't have looms."

"I knew that, but I'd forgotten. Then those men don't have secrets?"

"Of course they do. At least, I've never heard them talk about anything but business, so I suppose all the rest of their lives is secret."

Raím nodded tensely. "Forbidden."

"Not exactly. It's just that men and women don't talk to each other. I mean, they *flirt,* and once they're married they talk about money or the children or dinner. Things like that. But they don't *talk.*"

"Not about the work of their hearts," Raím said to the ground.

"What?"

"Nothing."

But Kat said, "You mean the work that you have

to do or die. Like what you said you wanted—to bring new patterns to your loom."

"You remembered what I said." Raím pulled on his lower lip. In a voice gruff with shyness, he said, "So what's the work of *your* heart?" Then he turned away, tossing pebbles into the darkness in front of his face.

"I don't know," said Kat. "And I won't ever know, because there's no time to find out. Everybody has to teach, teach, teach me until there's no time to be quiet and find out who I might already *be*."

"Suppose you found out who you were," said Raím, "and it turned out you were a monster?"

"I am a monster."

Raím straightened. "Don't make me laugh."

"I am! I'm half Leagueman."

"That's a piddling kind of monster. Not like me."

"You? You're insane, is all. Bashing doors, hurling cats."

"Brook asked for it!"

"He's only a kitten."

Raím hit the door frame with his fist. "This morning, while I was at the—on the mountain, *you* know where, that dear kitten pulled my spool rack over. Wrecked my yarns. Damn him—he's lain in the middle and kicked, he's turned somersaults and done the backstroke. He's drawn out all my spools."

"He was just playing."

"No doubt." Raím put his head in his hands and said through his teeth, "I can't find a yarn end anywhere. I'll have to ask Set for help. He's back from the hunt, and I'll have to listen to how terrific he was; I'm out of food, and now this."

Kat thought of Set's arrogant, unscarred face.

Raím lifted his head. "Why the hell should you like me?" he said. "I *am* a monster. I blinded myself. There's nothing left of me but secrets, and I can't show them to you. I yell at you, I can't hunt, and I have to ask my little brother to find my damned yarn end."

"It's true you're hard to like. You're all spikes, like a porcupine."

"A porcupine!"

"I know that's not as impressive as a blue serpent."

The kettle shrilled.

"Devil take you, you little chit," said Raím. He rose and went inside, leaving the door ajar. Kat heard his litany of curses as he made tea. She thought how Nall sang himself through his life, and Raím cursed.

But Raím did not bring the tea. Kat sat on the bench and swung her feet, watching the first bumblebees fumble in the sage. The cursing had stopped.

"Raím?"

No answer.

She turned to look at the door. Because it was half-open she had to look away. "Hey, Raím."

Still no answer. Brook came slithering along the wall of the bothy, making himself as tall and thin as possible.

"Raím! Here comes Brookie, trying to look invisible. He loves you anyway."

Raím came to the door. Brook streaked between his ankles, into the house. "Look," said Raím with an effort. "Kat. Would you come in?"

"*In?*"

"The tea's ready. Come in. If you want to." With his face turned away he said, "I'd show you my loom."

13

I CAN'T LOOK on your loom!

The words were on Kat's lips, but she did not say them. She saw Raím's face; it was stony, yearning, half-averted.

She said, "You mean it would be all right?"

"How the hell should I know? I'm supposed to see it, and I can't. You're not supposed to see it, and you can. That's fair."

"Why would you show me?"

Very low, he said, "If you think you like me you ought to know who I am. Some rotten weaver." He turned his back and went into the bothy, where he spoke from the dark. "I don't give a damn whether you come in or not."

Bian had asked, *Can you look behind the stars?*

Kat thought, No, but I can look behind a door. It's the same thing.

"I want to see," she said, and stepped over the threshold.

But she could not see. After the brilliance of day the bothy's darkness fell on her like a blanket. For an instant she thought she was blind, that Ouma's punishment had been swift. She flung out one hand and stubbed it on Raím's back. "It's dark!"

He chuckled bitterly. "Oh, you child of sunlight."

He dragged his staff from a corner and felt the ceiling with it, shoving upward. A rough board skylight fell open with a bang. Sunlight pierced down; Kat exclaimed again and caught Raím's sleeve.

"What's the matter?" he said, dropping the staff.

"A thunderbolt!" She put her hand over her eyes.

"Yes."

An image glared on her eyelids: a white lightning stab on a black ground. She dropped her hand, squinting, to look at what had branded her eyes.

She saw the reverse of its afterimage. On the white cloak that filled the loom from floor to ceiling, a black jagged bolt jabbed downward. Black lines shivered around it like ripples in the water around a hurled stone. It seemed bigger than the loom, bigger than the room that held it; in fact the loom was part of the room, its huge cedar beam pegged to the rafters and staked to the dirt floor.

Raím raised his arms and leaned both hands on a ceiling beam as though he, like the loom, were pegged to it. In a surly voice he said, "You like it?"

She did not like it. It was too strong to like. But she almost loved it, as she stood blinking and getting used to the cracking shock of light and darkness. She put her hand into the shaft of sunlight; it was pinky brown as a baby's against the lightning flash.

"And you can't even *see* it," she said.

"Tell me what it looks like."

She shook her head. He waited, biting his thumbnail. At last she said, "Maybe it's not for *any* eyes to look on?"

But she looked again and could see better what it was made of. The white wool was faintly creamy, like a lamb, and the black was rich and soft as bear-skin. "May I touch it?"

"Sure." His thumbnail bled. He scowled.

She stroked the taut cloth. It felt friendly, almost warm. Thousands and thousands of threads made up the whole.

She turned to him accusingly. "You know what to do to *make* this! If I could make something like this I would be happy for the rest of my life."

"Would you?" He reached out and rubbed the edge of the cloak between his fingers. "Then why doesn't making this make everything better?"

She said nothing. Brook came out from behind the loom, plumped down in the patch of sunlight, stuck one leg straight up, and began noisily to wash.

"Damned cat," said Raím. He turned away, grop-ing for the teakettle.

Kat marveled that he could be so homey in the same space as the loom. The smutty pot and two mugs with broken handles stood on the hearth next to a gnawed loaf. The bothy was even dirtier than before; scattered on the floor was the withered cooking trash of someone who could not see what he had dropped, and the pelts that were the bed were wadded like a laundry heap.

She found she was still clutching the jar of olive oil. She set it on the windowsill.

She looked around and saw, among the unfamiliar weaving tackle, Brook's havoc of yarns. Spools were unwound across the floor; the dull and bright blacks and whites that seemed to be Raím's favorites were matted and snarled.

She whistled. "So *that's* what the cat did!"

"Yes."

"I'll untangle it for you."

"I don't need your help!" Raím waved her away. The mugs of tea that he carried splashed and ran down his arms. He held one mug toward her, and she took it. "Oh, damn," he said, And in a formal voice, "It would be very good of you to help me with the spools. I would appreciate it very much."

"Raím," said Kat, "can't you ever—"

Then she shut herself up by drinking tea—smacking, because Brook was smacking as he washed his feet.

They drank without speaking, without sitting down. At last Kat put down her mug and stretched cautiously to look at the top row of weaving, where Raím had left off.

"You can't see the difference between black and

white," she said. "How can you make the design?"

"I spin the black yarn tighter. Here, feel."

He drew two threads into her hand.

She closed her eyes. "I can't feel any difference. But I could untangle the spools by looking. I'll do that."

"In a minute. I want you to know how my loom works."

She said shyly, "All right."

Raím spoke quickly, as though he was afraid she might run off. "This is the Sky Beam." He laid both hands on the huge crossbeam that hung from the rafter pegs. "Reach."

"It's too high!" said Kat, jumping. "I can barely touch it. I thought its name was the great beam."

"The Sky Beam is its true name. You've touched the sky." Raím ran his hand down one of the cedar uprights as though it were a horse's leg. "These brother beams—their true name is the Mountains. Touch them. And these threads—the warp—they're the Rain, falling down on the weaver as he works. The hearth loom weaves like the sun, from east to west, but the great loom weaves from earth to sky.

"The heddles' names are Night and Day. Where the heddles pull, that's where the weaving happens. Its name is the Dancing Ground. The yarn as it comes from the shuttle, before it's beaten in—that's the Deer Mouse's Tail."

Kat laughed. "Her tail shows in her track when she sits. I drew it on my pot."

"There's a story we tell in the Holds, how Deer Mouse runs away from his wife to work with Trouble and weaves his tail into the cloth. I'll tell it to you sometime. These heddle loops—here, give me your hand, you can feel them—their name is Trouble's Eyes. That's because he needed more than two, to watch for Ouma coming—What's the matter?"

Kat had pulled her hand away. She said, "Nothing. I just thought about how . . . you *are* telling me men's secrets. The true names."

"So what? The devil—I said I'm not a man."

Kat looked over her shoulder at the doorway that framed the Tells, now bright and golden green. "'The devil,' you said. Don't you think something might—"

"Punish us?"

"Yes."

"Like that thing that chased you?"

"Yes."

"Or the devil. Or Ouma herself."

"You believe in her. You wash your eyes in her spring."

"Is there a law against washing my eyes? And who knows for sure who that spring belongs to?" Raím picked up the batten and slapped it absently across his hand. "I told you on the cliff that it was I who chose to step on that rock. I haven't believed in punishment so much, since I fell."

"Why not?"

"Because I wasn't pushed."

A fat honeybee blundered in the open door, zoomed around them, and plunged out again into the light.

Very low, Kat said, "Maybe there's something older than Ouma. Maybe something made *her*."

"*What made these hills still hunts these hills*," said Raím.

"What?"

"That's a hunter's saying. These days they'll tell you it's about the bear, but my great-grandfather used to say it was about something older than Ouma. About what ate her."

"To make her a woman?"

"Yes," Raím said. "Women went up Dark Heart by themselves, before. They didn't need us to bring them their bears. Maybe then it didn't matter so much if a man . . . if a man couldn't hunt."

He rubbed his eyes. "Kat. I think if there's a mystery that's real, then it's too big to know. It's too pure to profane by looking, or by speaking names, or even by cursing. It's too strong to be broken by the likes of you or me."

His face was uncompromising. With a sigh Kat touched the batten in his hand. "All right. I know one name for this already. It's the cudgel."

He reddened, and said, "I won't tell you the true name for that."

"But it's not true that the cudgel sets everything in order, the way Emmot said. The order's already here—in the posts and the warp, and in the pattern you choose to weave. All the cudgel does is hit." With sudden understanding she said, "Creek's like that. The pattern's set up before you're born, and there's nothing left to do but beat it into place."

"Who taught you that?" said Raím.

"Nobody. Anybody can see it."

"Not me. Till now."

"Look," said Kat. "I mean listen. To make cloth you need some kind of loom, right? Otherwise it's a big tangle, like Brook's."

"A loom is just a frame to hold the threads as they go over and under. It keeps the tension. If I lose my tension I'm in trouble."

"But as long as you had frame and threads and tension, wouldn't there be lots of ways to weave?"

"Of course. I can use different yarns, or I can double weave, or change the patterns in the warp and weft. I can weave loops right into the fabric—hell, I can build a different style of loom altogether, and still make cloth."

"So there," said Kat. "I'm sick of hearing how things have to be. There are more ways to weave than anybody knows about, probably. That means there must be more ways to make water jars, and more ways to be a woman or a man."

Raím turned away, holding the batten in both hands. "Ways to be a man," he said.

Then he shook himself; he shoved the batten into the warp and left it there. To Kat he said, "Any stupid girl can make a water jar. But to see that Creek's a loom—the devil, Kat, you're amazing."

Kat was so flattered that she had to be stern. "We ought to start untangling this mess. Brookie, you bad cat, see the work you've given us?" She picked up Brook and scratched his belly. "Here, take him,

Raím. Tell him you're sorry you threw him out."

"I'm not sorry," said Raím. But he lifted the cat's wiry body against his shoulder, turning his face against the fur. "He's been roaming," he said, his voice muffled. "He smells wild—like wet grass and bees."

"Roaming—oh, Zella's goat!" Kat felt guilty, but only for a moment. "Well, I said I'd look for him, not find him. He'll be in the water meadows, or else by the millpond with the old white horse."

"That bony mare? I thought she was dead long ago. We used to ride her."

"The children still do. This morning they had her down in the cattails; they were climbing onto her back and falling off into the mud. They shouldn't. It's not warm enough." She watched the man rubbing his face on the cat's chest. "It looked nice."

"What did you play at when you were little?"

"I had a cat," she said. "But he got old. I never played in the mud. I never swam or danced. I don't think I ever *laughed*."

"I did all those things. I still came to the dark."

"I don't care," said Kat. "I would give anything, I'd give—"

"Don't say your eyes!"

"I want to be six years old, with bare feet. I want to fall off a big white horse into the mud."

"I want to see your face!"

"You can't." She could not bear the unfairness, for herself or him.

"Kat. Come here." Raím put Brook down carefully, on all four paws. "Sit on the floor, facing me. Feet here."

In front of the thunderbolt he began to slip off her clogs.

"What are you doing?" She tried to jerk her feet away.

"No, it's all right, Kat. Listen. I can't give you a white horse."

She stared. He pulled off her stockings. In his big hands her feet were small and warm, faintly crisscrossed with last summer's sandal tan.

"There," he said. "They're just as bare as when you were six."

With her face on her knees she whispered, "It's not the same."

"Borrowing your eyes to see my loom isn't the same as seeing it myself." He set her feet down carefully, as he had done with Brook. "But I'm damned glad of it. Now we need mud."

"Mud?"

"To fall into," he said, and his face was Set's—mischievous and wild. "You're the potter. Mud's your stuff."

"You're crazy!" she said, laughing.

He kicked off his own clogs and stockings. "All right, where's mud? The creek. Let's go!"

"They'll see us—anybody on the creek path!"

"You're right. Ah! There's rainwater in the barrel—come on, we'll make a wallow a hog would be happy in."

"Madman!" But she followed him. "Take the kettle to bail with!"

"Bail, hell." He was busy at the door. "I'll dump this over!" The round mirror of water in the rain barrel trembled and slopped, drawing itself a target of concentric rings.

"Not all at once!" squealed Kat. But Raím, laughing like a god of thunderbolts, rocked the barrel back and forth until the water burst in fans of diamonds—drenching himself, drenching Kat, drenching the dusty dooryard. Brook streaked for haven in a poplar.

"You want mud? I'm king of mud! I'm king of spring!" Raím hurled the barrel on its side; the hoarded water surged over Kat's ankles. Panting

and shining, Raím cried, "You want the creek? Just
ask me. The river? You want the sea?"

Kat laughed. The flying water drops were rain-
bows.

But the surf stilled. The barrel was empty. The
sandy silence, dull with the hum of bees, flowed in
again. Wiping his face in the crook of his elbow,
Raím flung out his arms and said, "Mud."

"It's clay." Kat worked her feet in the new pond.
She was cold, exhilarated, full of some sadness that
she did not want to look at. She pulled the folds of
her culottes between her knees, stirred the yeasty
water, slopped into it a fistful of red silt, and picked
out the twigs and stones. She slapped the muddy
disk between her hands like a corn cake. "Come
feel this."

Raím waded toward her gingerly.

She laughed. "Liar! You hate mud. Here." She
mashed the clay into a ball and dropped it into his
outstretched hand.

He pressed his thumb into the middle of it.
"*Women's* secrets," he said, grinning. "But I made
stuff of clay when I was small. I stopped when I
learned to toss a spindle."

Kat took the ball, slapped it flat, marked it with a

twig, and gave it back to him. "Tell me, what's that?"

Raím felt it with his forefinger. "Raven's footprint."

"Yes. This?"

"Deer-mouse track. You copied it from the shard."

"I copied it from the deer mouse! Wait." She pinched out a little figure, marked on it a whiskered face, and jigged it up his wrist, trilling like Brook.

"I can guess blind—it's a cat. Let me feel. Hup, the tail's come off."

"I'd have to fire it." Her face fell. "I don't think they'd let me do that." Looking at the crude little cat in Raím's palm, she said, "Sisira says I can experiment. Maybe. After I've gone to my bear."

Raím's red brows bunched. "Why should you go to your bear?"

"Because everybody does. Bian wants me to. I'm from Creek."

"You're not. You're a woman of the big world. What did you just tell me? 'There are more ways to weave than anybody knows about, and more ways to be a woman.' You're not some Creek wench!"

He shut his fist around the little cat. "Go to your bear, and then see if you still wonder what ate Ouma. See if you experiment. You'll be making jam jars for the whole town, the same design since

Ouma tethered Trouble's loom. The devil! You'll marry some lump of a hunter who doesn't have a thought beyond bear, bed, and breakfast; you'll nag him for sport. You'll be a woman then, by damn—see if you still chase your goats under the sky!" He opened his hand to show the clay shapeless, the marks of his fingers bitten deep. "See if you visit me then, or dare look on my loom."

"I'm not afraid of your loom!" But she remembered the eyes of the bear in harness, dark as a doorway, and did not know what lay beyond them.

"Kat." Raím blundered out his hand to find her shoulder. "Don't do it. Ouma *eats* you. Then there's no pattern but hers, and the rest of the world is shadow." He gasped for breath. "Kat, wild sparrow voice—stay free!"

She jerked away. "You don't know what it's like!"

A cheeky whistle rang from the far side of the bothy, followed by a voice that sang,

> Waiting by the creek.
> Maybe the doe comes.
> Oh, yes!

"All devils!" said Raím. "It's my brother!"

14

"SET!" SAID KAT in the same breath. She was tousled, barefoot. The forbidden loom stood beyond the open door, perfectly visible, her clogs and stockings in a heap in front of it. "What will he think about you and me?"

"Set only thinks one thing about men and women. Oh damn, and the loom!"

"There's no place to hide." She stared around at the skimpy sage, the poplars barely leafed. "Inside the bothy?"

"He'll want to see the weaving. And you stink of perfume!"

"Stink!"

"I could find you in the dark. I could find you in a goat pen—"

"This *house* is a goat pen. It's filthy—garbage on the floor, the bed's a pile of greasy—"

"Hide there!" Grabbing for her shoulders, Raím tumbled her through the door. "Get under the skins. You know how to hide from eyes!"

Snatching up her clogs and stockings, Kat said, "I bet there are *fleas*!"

"I hope they bite you!" He shook her. "Hide!"

She dove for the bed, burrowing like a mouse under the bearskins, sheepskins, pelts of antelope and wolf. The smothering dark was like the Bear House; she lifted the edge of the bearskin to get a breath.

In the bright rectangle of the doorway she saw Raím's body, blocking it as he used to block it against her. She heard Set's careless voice.

"Hey, brother, I'm back. Are you hungry yet?"

"Go to hell. You didn't shoot yourself in the foot?"

"Not likely. You survived, it seems. I killed well.

There's meat for you in the smokehouse; I'll bring it when it's ready. I clubbed a couple of hares this morning. They'll keep you till then."

"Toss them on the bench."

"With two throws of the cudgel I brought them down."

Kat saw Raím flinch. "Once I shot two rabbits with one arrow."

"It wasn't your marksmanship. It was what the rabbits were doing when you shot them." There was a thump on the bench as the hares were flung down. "You're a mess, brother. What's the barrel dumped for? I shouldn't leave you by yourself. How's the weaving?"

"Fine."

"Let me see it."

"There's nothing to see."

"The hell! I've been gone for weeks."

"What's on it isn't what I want," said Raím. "I'm changing it. I won't show you."

"What's on it is never what anybody wants. They're not happy about you at the Holds. And they're nagging at me because I buy wool for you— a pile of beaver skins I traded, in Ten Orchards."

"You'll sell the cloak in Ten Orchards when it's

done. You'll have half the money; hell, take all the money. Buy ribbons to bribe girls with. You'll see my weaving then."

"I want to know what I'm getting. Let me have a look. I'll tell you if it'll sell."

"I don't need your eyes!"

"Then don't eat my hares. Raím, I wear the serpent—I've got a right to look on your loom."

Kat dropped the edge of the bearskin. She heard a scuffle at the door, an angry exclamation, a laugh.

"Your arm's still strong," said Set, half admiring.

Raím's voice was genial with relief. "My god, little brother—you smell like a perfume merchant. How did you sneak up on those hares? Or did you just stand upwind and watch them keel over?"

"You used to wear perfume! Just because you don't need it now!"

"I never needed it. I got girls without it."

"So can I." Set sniffed heartily. "But I like it, and so do the girls. And I can afford it. My credit's good."

"You're cock of the barnyard by default. Don't forget it."

"You'd let me? The devil, Raím, you get harder to stand every day. Show me what you're doing. I'll cover for you at the Holds. Otherwise you know what will happen—the elders will come look for themselves."

There was a pause. Then Raím said with sullen carelessness, "All right. Come in—this place could use fumigation. One look I give you, then you can tattle to the elders, there's a lad."

Kat froze.

Feet entered the bothy.

"Oh, brother," said Set.

The silence was so great that Kat's breathing sounded to her like a tin bellows. She held her breath.

"Holy—" said Set. His footsteps moved back and forth in front of the loom. "Sweet brother, are you in trouble! Or Trouble's in you, more like." With reluctant respect he said, "You can weave. By damn! I couldn't do that, even if I could sit still so long. You call the lightning down out of the sky, and you can't even see it! You want to change this cloak? By god, the elders will make you change it." Then he said, "Don't, though. It's incredible, Raím."

From somewhere in the dark Raím's voice said huskily, "Thanks."

Set burst out, "It's almost like you could weave yourself new eyes."

"Wish I could."

Embarrassed by his own emotion, Set said, "Hell! Wouldn't that be great? You could weave us lots of money. You could weave a girl for your bed—or I could just bring you one of mine, like the hares."

"Be damned!" cried Raím. "I don't need your girls! I don't need your hares—stuff them down your gullet!"

"I was joking. You're touchy as a wolf trap, I could never talk to you. Look, the spool rack's down—good god, I never saw such a mess. Are you making or unmaking, brother?"

"None of your business. You've had your look, now get out."

"What did you do it for? You know it's me who'll have to rewind them. Was that why?"

"I'll rewind them myself."

"The devil you will. Let's see you do it. I'll sit here and watch." There was a scutter of footsteps, very near.

"Get away from that bed!"

Set laughed. "Why? You got a girl in it?"

"Get out. There are fleas, big ones." Hugging her clogs to her chest, Kat heard Raím pause and drawl, "Or no. I said it needed fumigation; please be seated. Get your bottom bitten. Nothing could please me more."

"I'm sure," said Set. "You live like a pig. It disgusts even *me*, and I've got a strong stomach." The footsteps went away. "Say—did you hear the one about the flea on the girl's knee? He takes one step and he says—Hey. What's this?"

"Get out. Don't tell me your jokes."

"What's this? The hell with the joke. What's this on the floor, a girl's stocking?"

There was a silence so loud and long that Kat heard her own ears ring in the smother of the skins. She felt inside her clogs. One stocking.

In a tight, mechanical voice Raím said, "I don't get it. The flea says, 'What's this on the floor, a girl's—'"

"The devil, brother! I mean there's a stocking on your floor. Here, feel it. Why is there a girl's stocking on your floor?"

"A stocking?" Raím's voice was puzzled.

Kat lay rigid. In her mind she saw Raím drawing the stocking through his fingers. In another second Set would think to look around the room, where he would see two mugs with tea leaves, a jar of olive oil, slender footprints in the dust.

"It's that girl's," said Raím. "It has to be."

"Ah!" said Set with an exploding sigh.

"Just before you got here," said Raím, "a goat came. Big stinking billy. Came right into the bothy. Must have tried to eat the spool rack, because over it went. The devil! I kicked him out of here and damned if I didn't hear him guzzling in the rain barrel. I shoved him off and the barrel fell over—soaked me. There was a girl chasing him. She shouted at me, the little chit! Maybe she was barefoot, carrying her clogs and stockings. Go look in the dooryard, brother. Tell me if there are footprints in the mud."

"I saw goat tracks." Kat heard a soft step to the doorway. Set said, "Tracks all over: goat's in the dust, barefoot girl's in the mud, and yours, too. How'd you get her stocking?"

"Didn't know it was here. The cat must have brought it in."

"Cats don't bring in anything but mice and birds."

"What do you think?" cried Raím. "That I'd bring a woman in here with the loom?"

"You wouldn't," said Set. He must have looked at the loom again, because he said, "Good thing you're blind! It'd make me nervous staring at that thing all day. Like having to listen to a shout that never stops. Could you tell who the girl was?"

"That Leagueman's brat. I know her voice. She's bothered me before—brings her foul goat to forage upwind."

"She saved your neck once, didn't she."

"She . . . she told you that?"

"She said I should be kinder to you."

"Damn you! Get out of my house!"

"Damn yourself!" cried Set, losing patience. "I'm sick of you! I can't say anything, so I'll say it all and devil take it. She's a sweetheart. A cub. Too bad you'll never see her. She's little, like a pussy-cat, and always angry. A foreigner. She's . . . scarred. I never had a woman before who was scarred. I want her."

"Get out! Get out!"

"Give me her stocking! I'll run after her and give it back."

"No!"

"Give it to me. Why should you want it? Because she held your hand once? Because she's the only woman in four years who's touched you?"

"I'll kill you!"

"You won't kill me. Give it here!" There was a scuffle, a crash, a grunt from Raím that was like a cry.

Slowly, as in a terror dream, Kat lifted the edge of the bearskin enough to see Set crouching over

Raím with one knee on his wrist, tearing the stocking from his hand.

Set was gasping, almost sobbing. "Why do you make me do this? You made yourself blind, damn you, now *be* a blind man! I wouldn't fight a cripple." He rose and sprang to the door. Turning back, he shouted, "I wanted a brother to hunt with. You ruined it for both of us."

His shadow blocked the light for an instant and then he was gone, running. The sound of his feet faded into the drone of bees.

"Raím!" said Kat. He lay so still. "Raím!"

He rolled over and sat up. She tried to kick away the skins; they were heavy on her, they smelled of man, of him. She threw them off and scrambled to him, put her hand on his forehead looking for blood.

He slapped her aside. "Get away. Get out. Go take care of somebody else!"

"I just—"

"I don't need anybody. I don't need you. He's got your stocking. Go get it."

"He hurt you!"

"No." Raím put his fists over his face. Then he pushed his hair back and stood up, staggering a little.

He put out his hand and found the woven cloak, held on to the edge of lightning. "I hurt him. You heard. I told you before that I chose this for myself. That means I chose it for everybody else, too. Everybody who has to . . . take care of me. I'm sorry. Damn, I'm not sorry, just get out and leave me alone."

She did not know what to do. At last she said in a small voice, "All right." Gathering up her clogs and stocking she stood in the doorway. "Raím. Thank you for letting me see your loom."

He had turned away, stroking the edge of the weaving with his left hand. At her words he reached up and wove his fingers into the warp that was tied to the Sky Beam; with one strong jerk he yanked downward.

The warp threads snapped and curled like fiddle strings. Kat cried out; the great cloak hung like a broken wing, one thick wrinkle laming the thunderbolt.

"Now we're the same," said Raím. "My work and I. Don't worry, I'll fix it. Just enough. It'll be almost usable."

Kat was crying. Raím said gently, "Go home," and she went, barefoot in the sand, following the tracks of Zella's goat.

🦎 🦎 🦎

The goat was at the water meadow. So was Set. He lay on his back in the short sedge of the bank, chewing a grass stem and staring moodily at the billy, who shook his beard among the milkweed.

When Kat saw Set she turned to run away. But he saw her at the same time and sat up; she was too proud and angry to retreat. She ignored him, wading into the shallow water crying, *"Alee! Alee!"*

Set said, "Kat!"

If he had shouted, "Hey, cub!" she would have been deaf to it. But he had never called her by her name before. Without meaning to she stopped and looked at him.

"Kat. Would you mind coming over here for a minute?"

His courtesy alarmed her. Slowly she splashed over to him, her clogs in one hand.

He pulled the stocking from his sash. Without looking at her he held it out and said, "This is yours. I mean, is it yours? I found it."

She looked at the stocking, seeing it in Raím's hand. "It's mine."

"Take it, then."

She took the stocking. Set's face was truculent. To

cover for Raím's story she said, "Thank you. Where was it?"

"In, I mean, near my brother's. I was at my brother's place."

"I was out there. My clog split and I took it off. I must have dropped my stocking. I was running. The goat knocked the barrel over—actually, your brother knocked it over, kicking the goat."

"Raím!" Set spoke the name like a profanity. "What a jewel." He threw away the grass stem. "Look, you don't know him, do you? I mean, you just helped him that time."

She felt her blush begin, telltale, uncontrollable. To make it a blush of rage she said, "He hates my goat! He screams at me!"

"He didn't use to be like that!"

"Before he fell?"

"Damn him to hell!" Set looked up at Kat. She felt as though a door had swung back, as when Raím had asked her to look on his loom. "I was a stupid little kid," said Set, "but he didn't care. He took me with him. He was better than anybody. You should have seen him, with his bow in his hand!"

Kat nodded. She was afraid to move, afraid

to breathe, for fear the door would shut.

It shut. A slow blush to match her own flooded Set's face. He dropped his eyes. Scowling, he began to hit the ground with the heel of his hand. "Sad story, eh? Even before . . . *that* happened. He got big and mean, and he'd take my girlfriends." In rhythm with his words, Set hit and hit. "And he always . . . beat me . . . at wrestling."

He straightened his shoulders. "Talking about my brother is wasted breath. Let's talk about you, you're prettier. What do you owe me for your stocking?"

"I don't owe you anything." Kat threw clogs and stockings on the bank and went back to the goat.

But the billy had grown wise. He sidled and pranced, nipping at the offered corn bread but staying out of reach.

Set watched. "Cub!" he said at last. "Tell me you need me! How else will you manage your goat?"

When she did not answer he took off his own clogs and waded into the shallow water, walking backward in front of her. "That goat's like me. The way to catch him is to be nice to him. Try."

"I don't *want* to catch you," she said. "I don't even *like* you."

He paused in his backward tracks. Across his face scudded a look of disbelief and childish hurt, quickly hidden.

It dismayed her. She did not care if she wounded Set. But it was horrible to wound the boy inside him, the one he had shown her. "You're nice," she said. "You're fine."

He swaggered his thumbs into his sash. "She doesn't like my mouth. I'll grow a mustache."

"Your mouth is fine. Set, I don't want a sweetheart."

"Is there something wrong with you?" he said, to pay her back for hurting him. "You aren't *that* kind of girl, are you?"

"What kind?"

He looked at her through narrowed eyes. Then he said with decision, "You're all right, kitten. It's just that nobody's taught you."

"Taught me! That's all anybody ever does!"

"I'll teach you. I'm good. Hey—I forgot, tonight's the dance! I'll teach you that."

"I'm not supposed to dance."

"You danced last summer, I watched you. You danced at the solstice and the harvest."

"Everybody dances then. Cubs don't dance the full-moon dance. I'm a cub." This self-betrayal was so enormous that she stopped, astonished.

"Well, aren't you the little granny," said Set.

"I don't want to dance with you!"

Again that flinching look crossed his face.

"Look, Set. I like you. Really. I just want—"

Puzzled, triumphant, he caught her above the elbows and brought his mouth down close to hers. "You crazy cub! You want me? You do, you know it. I'll teach you to be a woman. I'll bring you your bear."

"I have to ask for it first," she gabbled. "I haven't asked."

"You don't know what it is."

But he let her go. "When you ask for your bear you know who'll bring it. I'm the best hunter in Creek." He made a kiss in the air. "You'll love it, I promise. Look, for practice I'll bring you your goat."

15

"I WISH MOTHER would let you wear real clothes to the dances, instead of borrowing all over town," said Jekka. "That's a baby dress, but at least it's a party dress. You'll just have to look like a cub for a little while longer."

"She looks stupid," said Esangi. "That skirt was even short on Bo. She looks like a juggler's monkey."

With a scowl at Esangi's many petticoats, Kat said, "Better than looking like a carnival tent."

Jekka said, "Cousin, you could ask for your bear

anytime. Springtime's good. Your water jar's made, and by the holy, you know the songs; if I have to sing them with you one more time I'll throw up."

They were walking along the evening streets to the Hearthstone, just before moonrise. Jekka and Esangi wore their best dance dresses, stiff with embroidery; Jekka wore her green glass necklace.

They collected Mía at the next corner. She had so many petticoats that she had to walk well away from the wall. "Hello, cub," she said, staring at Kat's borrowed skirts. "When are you going to ask for your bear?"

"Soon," said Kat, to shut them up.

She was not happy. She thought of Raím; the thunderbolt seemed painted on her eye. The lively crowd that drifted through the streets of Creek felt like a river of ghosts.

A dull silver shine in the east marked where the moon would rise. Outside the walls, on the prairie, a wild dog yowled. Kat thought what it must be like to be a bear on the flank of Dark Heart, watching for the moon.

In a block or two Kos and Elanne joined them,

along with a crowd of little boys who were hitting one another and tossing their spindles.

Jekka hailed her brother. "Mamikimi!"

He made a furious face at her. "Don't call me that! That's baby!" He skipped and sidled, then rose at Kat's elbow, followed by fat Nammo, his best friend. "Ask her, Nammo," said Mamik.

"No."

"Go on."

"No!" Nammo giggled, but he said to Kat, "Did the bear rip your heart out?"

"No."

"Can we see the scars?"

"No!" said Kat, mortified.

"Was it big?"

"It was huge," Esangi said suddenly. "The hugest bear, black as night, with claws like daggers. Now get out of here, you little nits—don't hound her."

The boys ran off. Esangi said, "They're like sweat flies."

The streets grew more crowded as they drew closer to the square. A woman with an infant at her shoulder turned the child's face away and pulled up the corner of her shawl.

Jekka drawled, "Don't put a curse on that baby, Kat."

Elanne said, "It's Bo's old dress; it makes Kat look peculiar." As if for permission she looked at the older girls and then said shyly to Kat, "You could borrow *my* old party dress. If you want. I'm taller."

Mía reached over her skirts to bat Kat's curls. "Weird cub," she said.

Kat's heart swelled with solidarity. She could not walk close to Mía because of the petticoats, but she nudged Jekka and even smiled at Esangi, who scowled back.

"Don't look now," said Mía. "More flies."

The young men in their finery came swaggering out. They blocked the way. Elanne and Mía spotted their sweethearts and ignored them.

"Don't let the men know you want your bear," said Jekka to Kat. "They'll bury you in bears."

"That crowd?" said Esangi. "They'd bury her in chipmunks."

"Ho-o-o, sweethearts!" said a boy with a very young mustache.

"Ho, moss face!" Mía said at once. "Slap your lip, there's a centipede on it!"

Kat laughed. She was one of the group, with a

team to back her up. Though she could see Set in the crowd she felt poised and competent. When a bony youth with a polished batten in his belt cried, "Sweet peach in baby clothes, may I have a bite of you?" she shouted back, "Break your tooth on my hard heart!" and was delighted when Esangi grinned.

They ran the gauntlet of young men and came past the Bear House to the fire, witty with late comebacks. The little boys and girls were there before them, nattering like grackles. The older women had settled to chat. At a little distance the married men had built a second fire with a deer carcass roasting over it; there they stood and spat, reliving past hunts and talking in low voices about the anatomy of looms.

The drums and flutes began. "I can't stay with you," Kat said to Jekka.

It had never distressed her before. Uninitiated young people did not dance at the full moon, but she had loved to stand with the married women, shy and awed, watching the young couples spin in twos—Elanne with Robik and Mía with Ailem, then trading and changing—while the little children did their best imitation with heel and toe.

But now she said to Jekka, "I wish I could come with you."

"Cousin, you need your bear. You do. Watch this time, and maybe next month you'll join us." With a rustle of skirts she was gone, leaning to Mía's ear over the petticoats and whispering some private joke.

Kat went to join the older women. Bian, who was in the middle of a debate about how to get an owl's nest out of a chimney, patted her shoulder absently.

Kat sidled to the edge of the crowd nearest to the men's fire. Muttered words and fragments of male stories drifted to her over the music, but even by leaning sideways she could not really hear.

She looked up and saw Emmot staring at her with a worried, warning look. Pretending nonchalance, she moved back among the women.

Wenta the headwoman saw her and asked Bian loudly, "When will our cub be ready for her bear?"

"When she asks for it," said Bian, "as we agreed."

Kat pretended not to hear. She watched the children dance. Nammo was being steered across the sand by a blond girl taller than he was.

"It's all right if you don't know how," said the girl. "I'll do the dance part, and you can kind of stand there."

"I'll do the dance part," said Set's voice in Kat's ear. "Step up onto my feet, sweetheart, and I'll sweep you away."

"I'm not six," said Kat. But she was glad to see him. He was so big and blithe, wiping his hot face and steaming like a dog on a cold morning.

"I'm not six either," he whispered. He slid his hand down her arm. "Come along, darling. I'll teach."

"Here now," said Wenta. "Grandson, you're not to dance with children."

"Are you a child?" Set asked Kat, tugging on her wrist. "*Are* you?"

Kat caught a glimpse of Bian's worried frown and opened her mouth to say, Yes, I am.

But the words would not come. Instead she took a step after Set, slackening the tension on her wrist.

"Ah!" said Set.

Wenta said, "You impudent cockerel!"

"Let them go, grandmother," said Bian, coming to the rescue. "The cub has been so good—and in those silly clothes. One dance, one dance only."

"She has not gone to her bear!"

Set wheedled. "It won't be a dance. Just a lesson. Right here, you can watch us."

Bian put her hand on Wenta's arm. "It's only

your little grandson. One dance, for joy."

Swollen like an angry hen, Wenta said, "Teach her, then. But not with the others by the fire. And respectfully! Young Set, see that you don't invite the same curse as your brother!"

Set pulled on Kat's wrist, not gently, so that she stumbled after him a yard or two. He turned his back on the women. "Damned biddies!" he whispered. "'Little grandson'!" Kat jerked her wrist away, but he caught it again, his face bright with anger and challenge. "So you want to dance?"

"Yes."

She said it so coolly that he was disconcerted. "I thought you didn't know how."

"I don't."

He recovered his cockiness a little and took her around the waist. "You've got the right teacher. Tuck your fingers under my sash, darling. That's right. Here we go." And as the other dancers began to turn and stare, he swung her into the first balancing steps of the full-moon dance.

That is, he tried to. He did not know how to teach.

"All right," he said. "Watch my feet."

Kat's head came only to the middle of his chest. She craned out to look, but her eyes could not tell her ankles what to do. She kicked his shins.

"No!" He was amused and annoyed. "Watch. Like this."

He showed her, holding her at arm's length. Stiff with concentration, she put her feet where he pointed. He stepped on them. *"Ow!"* she said.

"Oh, come on!" Set lost his slight patience. "Dancing's easy. What's the matter with you? Just *dance.*"

With all Creek watching, they turned in a jerky circle, bumping their knees.

A boy whistled from the fire. "He-e-ey, Set, can I have lessons?"

The young women followed it up with, "Teach her, don't squash her!" and "Get her a bear, it's safer."

"The devil!" hissed Set, and Kat hissed back, "Pigs! They should mind their own business."

"We'll show them," said Set. "Leave it to me."

He caught her up. There was nothing to do but grab for his neck as, his impudence restored, he whirled her in a circle in the firelight.

"Set!" she squealed as her feet swung wide.

He was laughing, his face as full of mischief and energy as Raím's had been when he rocked the rain barrel. "Dance with me, cub! Fly!" he cried, until

Kat was laughing too, laughing harder, feeling his long arms safe around her, seeing the night sky and its constellations spin around him as around the Navel Star.

He set her down. Still laughing, she staggered and caught his shirt front as the fire, the square, Bian, and the old women tilted like leaves on fast water.

He put his hand over hers on his chest and pulled her up against him. He turned to be sure he was seen, and in front of all Creek in the firelight and the moonlight, he kissed her hard and long.

"*Young Set!*" cried Wenta.

Kat stood dumbfounded.

"Run home to mama," said Set. "I count the days until your bear."

He faced her around and gave her a nudge. In five steps Bian had caught her hand and was saying between laughter and exasperation, "That boy! If he were a son of mine I'd beat him, never mind how big he is."

"The little chicken hawk," said Wenta, pleased that her judgment of Set's character had been correct.

The square tilted back to normal; the fire burned straight up. Set was dancing with Mía, gracefully, without a glance in Kat's direction. Matrons and children stared at Kat. She felt as naked as she had in the Bear House. Shamefaced, she ducked back away from the fire onto the cool, trodden sand of the open plaza.

No one followed her. So she was alone when she saw, in the black shadow of the granaries, Raím.

He leaned motionless on his aspen staff. His head was bent toward the distant music, the laughter and talk. Over the walls behind him the wild dogs, crazy with moon, sang their falling song.

He stood like stone.

As did she. He seemed to look straight at her, his face hard as a season without rain. Cry! she wanted to shout at him. Why can't you cry for your loneliness, for all your dancing lost?

But Set's kiss had soaked her, it stood out around her like Mía's petticoats. She could not go near Raím.

She took soft steps backward, toward the crowd. She saw him stir as though some spell were broken, rub his eyes, then turn northward down the alley, toward the Tells.

16

"I SAW YOU LAST NIGHT," said Kat. "Did you see me?"

Raím ignored this stupidity and shook his head. He was hunched on his bench at the bothy door, wearing nothing but his sashed kilt, the snake tattoo, and Brook, who prowled from one shoulder to the other. Kat led Zella's wicked goat by a length of rope.

Raím said, "You didn't come talk to me."

"You were leaving. It was too late to catch you. Why didn't you come to the fire?"

"To that madhouse? I can't stand it."

"It was nice." She swung the rope and the billy

sidled, clacking his wooden bell. "It's nice this morning, too. I ran here."

She had gone straight to Zella after breakfast, saying right out, "I'm not potting today. Give me that wicked goat and I'll take him to graze up the creek—he'll be so fat he won't chase the nannies." Zella had chuckled and said, "That's not how it is, dear, but take him—and bless you."

Outside of town Kat had felt her breath unfold. To mountain and prairie and enormous, wind-ridden sky she had shouted, *"Alee, alee!"* and urged the billy to a run.

Jackrabbits bolted, pheasants burst from the sage. A hawk shifted planes in the air to hang like a star at a safer distance.

As she passed the Tells she grew less sure of herself, thinking of the old brown skull. That woman had been alive once. Perhaps it had been on a spring morning that she went up Dark Heart, lonely, to meet whatever waited for her.

Kat ran a little faster, until she could see the line of poplars.

Shyness stopped her. Then she saw Raím, unmoving on the bench. With a strange leap of her heart she had cried, *"Alee!"* and had borne down on him, sending Brook to his shoulders as though up a poplar trunk.

"Phew," was all Raím said now. "Tie that beast downwind."

"It's me you smell. No perfume this time."

"The devil. Tie yourself downwind, then." He waved toward the dooryard, now patterned with footprints hardened in dry mud. "There's no water to wash in."

"It'll rain tonight and everything will be green. The badgers are out of their burrows, all busy. They say the bear's come out of her den."

She stopped. Raím said nothing, slumped in the sun. The bothy door was open; he made no attempt to close it.

"Raím, the thunderbolt is gone!"

"I cut it off the loom." The cedar frame was visible in the shadows—enormous, empty.

"You said you'd fix it."

"I don't want to fix it. I'll make something new."

He tossed Brook down. The cat streaked up a poplar to get away from the goat, and Raím leaned his elbows on his knees.

He said to his feet, "I want to weave something for you. Shut up. I know you won't like it and you won't use it and I'm a blind cripple, but I'm a good weaver and I can do what I want."

Sunlight, like vision itself, poured over him. He held out his hand like a beggar, then made a fist. "So don't nag me about it, all right?"

"Raím—"

He sat up straight and mimicked her. "'Oh, Raím.' What kind of stinking sentiment is that?"

She said nothing.

He kicked his clog in the dry mud. She took the goat to Brook's poplar and tied it up. When she came back he said, "You don't really know what sunlight feels like. You only see it." Then, almost inaudibly, "Did you get your stocking back?"

"Yes."

He was silent. She could not look away from his face, and suddenly did not care. She wanted to look at him, into him—to look and look and look.

"You're pale in the daylight," she said. "Raím— you're like me, you even have freckles on your lips."

"You have freckles on your lips?"

"I have freckles *everywhere*. When I was little I tried to scrub them off with lemon soap."

"It worked," he said. "I don't see any freckles."

She sat down on the bench beside him. "Want

to buy some lemon soap? I know a Leagueman."

"You silly chit." He leaned away from her. "What's it like there? In the Leaguemen's land."

"It's not their land. They just drive their mules over it." Kat leaned her chin on her hand. "The wind blows all the time there, and the sea is everything."

"You mean big?"

"Yes. When I first came here I missed the sea, but not anymore. Here stone and sand are the sea, the earth is water. When the badger burrows he swims in the earth."

Raím lifted his hand outward, as though he could feel space. "When I had eyes I hardly looked at this, my home. I hardly noticed. But you can go back to your own place, and see."

"Yes."

"Will you?"

"I suppose so." She stared out at Dark Heart. "I didn't want to go back until I'd gone to my bear."

"If you go to your bear you'll stay in Creek."

"Maybe. I don't know."

He sat with his head bowed. The goat bell clonked at the edge of the yard.

Kat said, "Set would bring me my bear."

"I know."

"Set has nice legs," she said, to goad him from his stony hunch.

"He kissed you. Sure he did."

"I didn't ask him to."

"You liked it."

She said, "I liked it that I wasn't so hideous that *nobody* would kiss me."

"You're crazy! Who wouldn't—"

"You don't even know how I look."

"The devil! I don't need to!"

She pulled up her knees and put her face on them. "You can't see what the bear did. But I can."

"Oh, hell," said Raím. "Don't cry, Kat. Sweetheart—"

"Why not? Because *you* can't? You men are stupid, you march around all brave and stiff."

"All right. Have a nice cry." He groped for her shaking shoulder. Patted it. "You had a nice time at the dance, now didn't you? Did you dance?"

"I can't. Set tried to teach me and I couldn't learn."

Raím snorted. "Set's patience is a dandelion clock—gone in a breath."

"I'm clumsy."

"The devil! You run in the dark. In the hills you don't stumble. Be damned, woman, if you're clumsy then I'm a Leagueman."

She imagined him as a Leagueman, grim in a black hat; she hiccuped, laughed, and swung her feet. "They wouldn't let you be one. Brook would pester the mules."

"That's better." He patted her again to reward her for not crying. "Look, I—I'd teach you that dance." Before she could refuse he said, "I don't dance anymore. I used to try, by myself, but it's not like the trail—I have my stick there and I can pay attention. When I dance I . . . forget, and then I hit something and fall down."

"You couldn't teach me, then."

"You could be the eyes. I know the rest." He stood up and held out his hand. "The devil. There's nobody to see us but that stinking goat. I'll teach you the easy part." He turned to her and said, "You can be stupid with me. Because I know you're not."

She rose and gave him her hand.

He led her over the crackling mud to the center of the dooryard, clear of buckets and stones, and laid his hands on her narrow waist. He said with wonder, "Such a small woman to hit me in the eye. Take hold of me."

Shyly she tucked her fingers under his sash, where the blue serpent raised its head and tail.

"The moon's past full. We'll dance to a goat song, that's the same measure." He began to hum, hunting for the tune. His humming tickled her palms, like a cat's purr. She looked at his feet, waiting for them to do something difficult.

But he was only shifting his weight like the bear, absently, and shifting her with him.

> *Alee, alee,* my little spotted goat *ala.*
> *Alee, alee,* my nimble yellow goat *ala.*

She forgot to be shy and rocked with him, singing, "*Alee!*" When he deftly swung her a quarter turn she came along with a squeak, settling again to rocking with a different view past his shoulder.

She laughed out loud.

"Not so bad, then?" He smiled, a real smile. He sang on until she had gotten the rhythm again and then swung her another quarter turn. "*Alee, alee.*" Slowly the turns grew frequent, never fast. With a few words he taught her how to place her feet, returning to rocking when she stumbled.

"*Me-e-eh*," said Zella's goat, and suddenly they were dancing, turning lightly over the ground. Kat steered them away from bench and barrel and stones; at her touch on his back Raím turned as simply as if she had sent a thought. Looking up at his face she saw it for the first time peaceful, marked by neither anger nor hunger. The hawk in the air returned, and the mountain full of bears swung around them. "*Alee, alee.*"

They spun more slowly, like falling leaves. Then they were only standing, in the plain dusty dooryard that smelled like goat. Kat took her fingers from Raím's sash.

He stood without moving. Then with a shudder he put his hands to his eyes and said, "I can't see! Where's my house? I'm turned around."

She caught his wrist and pulled him to the bench by the wall. He stumbled and clung to it. "Don't go," he said. "I can't—"

"Hush." She was afraid. "Everything's the same." The sun shone sturdily. Brook glared from the tree. She laid her hand against his cheek. "It's all the same as it was."

He said, "I flew."

"Yes."

"Kat." He let go of the bench and touched the hollows under her eyebrows, the parting of her mouth. "Kat, is this you?"

"Yes." She leaned forward and kissed his freckled lips. "Raím," she said, and put her arms around him.

17

"MY KAT."

His voice was like a breath, almost inside her ear. His arms were around her; his hands stroked her back. The wind smelled like melting snow.

She made a sound like a sleeper's whimper, putting up her hand to push away his mouth.

He kissed her fingers. "My lark," he said. "My mouse." Her new body ran to him like rain to the creek. "I love you," he said.

On the horizon an enormity was gathering. What had happened? Did she love him?

She thought, I must love him. I kissed him.

His big hand did not shrink from the scars. "Raím, no," she said. But she had given him her mouth; that must mean he could take anything he wanted. "No!"

He did not hear her. Then he heard her and laughed, fear in his face. "Don't you love me?"

"I love you."

She tried out the words. It was she who had led him on; she would have to see it through. She forced herself to touch the little springing hairs at his neck. They were gold.

Something in herself had drawn to her this man with his big shoulders and hard cheek. Because she had always been powerless this new power was awesome, and she could not give it up.

Set wants me too, she thought. Her hand of its own accord stroked the shape of Raím's throat. But when he returned his hand to her breast she said, "No," again into his mouth.

He drew back, alarmed. "Why not?"

"I don't want . . . I don't like it." But she did want, did like. And didn't.

"My speckled kitten."

"No!"

"Have you never kissed a man?"

"No." Never, except for Set's hectoring kisses.

Almost never.

In that instant, like a thunderbolt, she remembered Nall.

"Raím." She strained away from him. "Let me go!"

His long face shone with tenderness. He gripped her arms above the elbows. "I won't hurt you. I swear I won't. I'll make you a woman. You kissed me!"

It was true. She could think of nothing but to get away from him—to get somewhere to be safe from herself. Putting both hands on his chest, she said, "It's too soon."

"Too soon? Four years?" He grappled her to his body. "Waiting in the dark for four years?"

"Don't hurt me!"

"I would never hurt you." But he pinned her arms.

"For you it's four years." To buy safety she bartered her adulthood, making her voice childish and weak. "It's so strange for me. I'm scared."

"I can teach. You know that. Let me teach."

She said nothing.

"The devil!"

But he dropped his hands. She stood up between his knees. He laid his cheek against her breast, put his arms around her waist, and swung her gently, saying with desperate hopefulness, "*Alee, alee.* Remember that, my goat girl?"

"Raím, I want . . ."

"Anything."

Anything to make him let her go. "I want to go slow. Like the dance, the way you taught me."

"You liked that, didn't you, kitten? I can be patient. For you I'll be patient."

"Raím, let me go."

He held her culottes bunched in his fists.

"Raím."

He let her go. With his hands on his thighs he strained to see her, his eyes fixed where he thought her face must be. "I love you," he said.

"I love you."

It was true. And she hated him and feared him, and loved Nall. She had even loved Set a little, when he swung her in the firelight, and when he had shown her his sad boy's face by the water meadow.

Her father was right. She was a slut, attracted to any man. Bian was right too: the world was too crazy to endure without rules. She could not even govern herself.

She touched Raím's face. He did not move. As she slipped beyond his reach he raised his head.

Shaking, she untied the goat, forcing her fingers to hurry at the knot.

"Kat, where are you?"

"I'm going home," she said, her voice breaking. "I'll come back. I'll come as soon as I can."

"Kat!"

She freed the rope, yanked at it, and ran stumbling toward Creek, the billy with his bell clacking alongside. Where the green hummocks of the Tells rose up beside the path she turned and called back wildly, "Good-bye!"

18

BIAN WAS YANKING up weeds. She sang an old song about a hoe, and the hens followed her, scratching for worms. When Kat slipped through the garden gate Bian sat back on her heels, smiling, wiping her forehead with the back of her hand.

"I pull and pull," she said, "but there are more of them than me. And they are so much younger."

"Bian," said Kat.

Bian narrowed her eyes. "How is my cub this windy morning?"

"Bian, I want my bear."

"Oh, daughter!" Bian's joyful face changed to shining compassion. "Who is it, little one? Is it Wenta's grandson?"

Kat's blush began—the wretched blush that strangled her like a stutter. But for once she could be honest with a word.

"Yes."

"I thought so. Look at that face, the cat that ate the pudding! What happened?"

"Nothing."

"Nothing you'll tell me, and that's as it should be. I'm a snoopy old woman. Oh, sister's child, it's your time and your lad, but it makes me happy."

"Bian. How soon can it be?"

"As soon as you want." Bian trudged over, her clogs heavy with mud, and put her arms around Kat. "Have you fallen so hard?"

Kat held her face against Bian's shoulder, thinking of a hard fall into the dark. Then she thought of Nall and said, "Bian—in my old home there was a man. . . ."

"So there's the trouble." Bian stroked Kat's hair with hands that were not Raím's. "Dear child, you'll love him always. But it will be like remembering spring, once summer comes. Look how much you've grown this year, how much you've suffered! You'll be a woman, ready to govern a man of your own people."

"I'm only half from Creek."

"You're all Creek. You're the bear cub, the mountain rose. You're Lisei's daughter; the rest of your making was only a man."

With her rough earthy hand she led Kat indoors, calling for Jekka. Emmot at his hearth loom gave Kat one of his slow smiles.

"This girl is going to her bear," said Bian.

"Aunt!" Couldn't she just get it over with and be safe, without announcements?

Emmot stretched, cracking his back. "Right, then. Who's the lucky fellow?"

"Don't tease her. She doesn't have a leathery hide like you." Bian nudged her husband with affection and contempt.

Kat thought, They love each other. I guess.

Jekka came in from mending the back fence. "Is there a fire, Mother? You're screeching like a crow."

"A fire at the Hearthstone, for a bear ceremony."

Jekka whooped and whacked her hatchet into a log in the wood box. "When?"

"As soon as may be. I'll gather the Circle right

after I wash, and Emmot will call the hunters."

Emmot hung up his loom and put his pipe in his back teeth. "You'll have your bear," he said, and sauntered into the sunshine.

Bian left. Jekka cornered Kat by the stove. "You *have* to tell me. He kissed you again, didn't he?"

"Jekka—"

Kat thought to tell the truth. Maybe Jekka would know what to do. But her cousin caught her by the waist and swung her in silly circles, chanting, "I *said* I'd give you my *neck*lace and I *will*!"

Grabbing at bits of the incomprehensible world that spun by her, Kat said, "Will I have to get married right away?"

"You're cra-a-azy! What did I do for fun before you came? He'll just be your sweetheart. Cousin, he's so handsome! Just be careful you don't get a baby with him."

"Wait," said Kat, with a feeling of whirling out of control. "What do you mean?"

"We teach you the mysteries right after the bear. It takes your mind off the tattooing." Jekka stopped her dance. Her face grew serious and she looked, for a moment, very like Bian. "The answer to all the questions in the world is: join the Circle, and little by little the questions answer themselves."

If I drew the circle small enough, thought Kat, I could understand everything in it.

That sounded safe. The room no longer spun around her but stood like a rock, a tree. She remembered how sufficient this warm house had felt last year. She said suddenly, "I miss my father."

"Your *father*? Why should you miss him?"

"I wish he could tell me, 'Good luck.'"

"I'm not hungry."

"Sister's child, you must eat. Nothing for two days—it's not good. You'll have three days' fasting before the bear."

"I'll be sick if I eat," Kat said rudely. She was on her knees, polishing the hearth hard with a raveled sock. "Don't call me 'sister's child'!"

Bian slid the offered plate back onto the table and knelt beside her. "Kat. Are you pregnant?"

"*No!* How can you ask that? What do you think I am?"

But there was nothing to protest. She was a slut. She burst into tears, clutching the sock.

"Sweetheart, I didn't mean that."

"Don't call me names!"

225

"Kat. Be still." Bian put her arms around Kat's shoulders. "I didn't mean to offend you. It's just that you eat nothing and seem so hurried and distressed. I thought maybe you had made love with Set. It's not wise, daughter, but it's no sin. Many of us come into womanhood a step ahead of ourselves."

"I didn't!"

"I believe you. Is it Set you're fretting for, off in the wilderness? Or just all of it, the bear?"

"It's the heat," sobbed Kat.

For it was hot, a chalky, unseasonable heat like the air in a closed box. The promised rain had not come. The chickens muttered and lagged in the shadows. Even the flies buzzed slowly. Heat rippled the poplar spears.

"It's like this every spring—two weeks of misery until our bodies remember how to be hot. Think of Ouma in her fur coat!" Bian patted Kat's back. "Go lie down. Sleep like the owl until the cool night comes."

"I don't want to lie down."

Kat had not slept well either, for two nights. If she slept Raím might come, groping his way to her in the dark, and she would dissolve into his arms again; or Set would come with the bear, and take her before she was armed against him. Vigilant, she had to keep herself until the bear could keep her. "Why do they take so long? It's been two days!"

"It took them four days to bring your first bear."

What Emmot had promised he had done quickly. By midnight of the first day a party of men with nets and cudgels were gathering by the Loom Holds. Kat had known it only by a song in the alley, low but sweet:

> Waiting at the window,
> Maybe the girl comes.
> Oh, ycs!

Because she had been lying awake Kat heard it before Jekka, who slept curled up like a hedgehog with her pillow over her head. She had sat up in bed and pulled the curtain back, seeing the waning moon like a bowl turned over for the kiln.

"Shhh! Get away!"

"Come to the gate, then." Even Set's whisper was big. "Or I'll sing loud."

She drew the curtain.

"*Waiting . . . ,*" Set sang.

Kat opened the curtain. "All right. Stop."

His teeth flashed white as he turned to pad

around the house. She rose in the dark. The unbolted kitchen door swung wide, swung shut.

At the gate she said, "If you touch me I'll scream till the village wakes."

Set leaned on his long bear cudgel. "I won't touch you unless you ask me to. Ask."

"No."

"I'm going to get your bear." He rubbed the scar on his thigh. "This was for you last time, darling. What do you owe me?"

"Nothing."

"One kiss. After your bear I'll give you twenty."

"No."

"For luck! My brother's cursed me, I need luck." She drew in a breath. "Raím."

"It irks him when he can't bring a girl's bear."

"You told him it was for me."

"This afternoon I took him his rabbit and the news, and he cursed me. Come on, you can't send me to your bear like that."

"I'm not sending you."

"But I'm going. For you." He touched his scar again. For once his voice was serious and hard. "You belong to me. Ouma marked us both. Kiss me and send me to your bear."

228

What did it matter? The bear would eat her. She took his shirt in her hand, pulled his face down, and kissed him on the mouth.

"Hey!" He laughed and caught her arms. "That was proper. Give us another."

"You said one kiss."

"Fair enough." He let her go. "You little fox! I knew you knew more than you'd show. Wish me luck, darling."

"Good luck," she said, to make him go away. Then she crawled back over Jekka's feet and lay in the moonlight, watching the blade of shadow eat her body under the thin cloth.

Now in the heat of this second afternoon Bian was saying, "You're keyed up, and no wonder. Go to the Clay Court, busy yourself in the shade. Get my stone and grind paint; that's eased better women than you or me."

No one was at the Clay Court. Inside the shed it was too hot to bear, so Kat pulled Bian's grinding stone from the shelf and carried it outdoors to the blue shade of the eaves.

The work did quiet her. The rhythmic leaning into the stone was like kneading bread or clay, the cadence of a song that for a moment could contain her.

But to think of songs was to think of Nall.

She stopped grinding. The stone was glossy, black, powdered with red. She had seen one like it somewhere.

Then behind her she heard it: the rattle of brown bones.

With a scream she jumped up and ran out of the Clay Court, down the alleys, turning left and right until she came to her own gate.

Mamik was swinging on it. "Here she is," he called over his shoulder. To Kat he said, "I saw your bear! She's *huge*! All black!"

"Hush!" Jekka grabbed his sash and used him like a handle to pull open the gate. "You're not supposed to tell her. Cousin, it's time! They got a fine bear. Get dressed, we'll go to the Blessing Tree for water."

"Is Set—"

"Smug as a cat, with a new scar. He'll bait you by the Loom Holds, don't fret."

"I won't go past the Holds!"

"Yes you will. You have to. Get dressed, I'll brush your hair."

When the girls had carried their jars to the Loom

Holds, in the low orange light Kat's hair shone like burning sage around her white face. The young men nudged one another.

"He-e-ey, cub! What'll you light with that torch?"

"Quench me, water girl!"

Kat held the perfect jar upright with one hand. She did not answer even when Set, carrying his newly bloodied arm like a medal, cried, "Your bear's hugged me, darling—now I know how."

"You're the cool one," Mía said as the young men parted ranks and the girls ran through. "Like a princess." They walked along the path and crossed the creek in the hot, blank air.

At every turn Kat thought to meet Raím. But the banks were empty. So was the meadow. On the knees of Dark Heart the Blessing Tree stood lonely, fluttering its ribbon prayers.

At the brink of the pool the grass was wet. "A fox has been teaching her kits to drink," said Elanne. "Kat, will you leave an offering?"

Kat felt at her neck for the blue beads. The thread had broken; they were gone. The beehive hummed, awake. "I already gave it all," she said.

But her eyes were on the rooty cave at the tree's

foot, above the pool. At the mouth of the cavern, hanging by its handle from finespun yarn, a broken mug revolved slowly. Kat saw the deer-mouse track.

She thought: It wasn't a fox that came here.

She knelt as though she were praying. But it was only to feel the earth, to be sure she was not falling.

Jekka sang,

> Out of the first place,
> Little river,
> Blood beginning,
> Over and over.

Jekka and Mía, Esangi, Sara, Ruma, and Kos jumped from stone to stone, dipping their jars; then Elanne and Bárteme, Arra, Gaími, Gel, Selem, and little Bo.

And Kat. Over she leaped, nimble as Zella's goat, and stood on the far bank with her jar full.

"Let's go," she said. "I want it to be time."

"That's not what you wanted before," said Esangi. "You've changed."

They came back as night washed the heat downstream, and left the jugs in the portal of the fasting hut. Old, deaf Kiku was raking the floor and laying the fire. The dark rose like water. Lamps were winking on. The girls crossed over to Creek and scattered homeward, calling, "Good night!" in high voices. Kat and Jekka turned in at their gate.

Bian stood beside it. "Inside, Jekka. I've made raspberry cake to tempt my nervous cub. Go get it out of the oven while I soothe her."

Jekka laughed. "You made raspberry cake for *me* before my bear. I thought about it for three days' fasting."

The door banged behind her.

Bian turned to Kat. "What's this about Raím?"

The world swung a quarter turn. "Raím?"

"He came to the gate, rapping with his stick. An hour ago. Asking for you."

Kat gasped. "What did he say?"

"Little. He was distraught. Only did you live here, and where were you? I warned him off. He knows better than to bother a girl before her bear. 'Wenta's grandson'! Is that where you went with the goat? Oh, Kat, what have you done?"

"I haven't done anything!"

But she could not even breathe without doing something. She could not live without having to make choices, every instant of every day—and she understood none of it. None.

"Bian," she cried, "I need my bear!"

"That you do, my cub," Bian said grimly. "Until now I didn't know how much. Three days—three days and you are safe."

19

A DAY IS THE TIME between dawn, when the sky gets white and the owls stop crying, and dusk, when twilight goes purple and the nighthawks thrum. A day is the time when wild dogs do not howl. There had been three of those times at least, she thought, and many, many nights. The days were hot, the nights were cold, but since she sweat and shivered constantly she confused them. The fire sank and she fed it, having nothing to feed herself.

For this Kat was glad. No food meant no body; no body meant no loving or longing, no pain. As the moon shone down the smoke hole she watched her breasts and thighs wane with it, growing each night more slender and remote. She would hardly feel the teeth of the bear.

She would refuse both Set and Raím coolly, like a princess; she would go back to her old home beautiful in her bones—bones were the only things that lasted—and Nall would love her.

The women in bearskins came and she sang with them, perfectly. When they left she raked the red dust smooth over their footprints, drank from the perfect jar, and settled back onto her knees. Kiku snored. Three days—the earth turned like a sleeper—three nights were almost over, like one held breath.

Pass, she told time silently. This instant is worthless. Hurry that future when I will be fed, be loved, be wise.

The fire burned out. The jar was dry. Kat looked at it; she saw the pattern of the Bear's Eye, a perfect circle small enough to be safe in. Her hand reached out and lifted the jar lightly, feeling how deliciously frail its walls were, scraped thin.

She opened her hand. The jar fell simply, like a bird's egg from a nest.

Old Kiku muttered in her sleep. Kat picked up a glassy shard and looked at the blue veins in her wrist.

She turned her hand over. Neatly, like painting the Bear's Eye, she made a long cut on the back of her hand, from the first knuckle to the base of her thumb.

It hurt. She was surprised. It was a numb, chill hurt; the gash was not shallow, not deep—an open mouth. Blood welled out in splashes.

So that's all there is to it, she thought.

She turned her wrist back to her blue veins and sat looking at them, the shard in her hand.

She knelt so motionless that under the door of the fasting hut crept a mouse.

It was a deer mouse. She thought herself unseen. Tiny, food for every larger creature, she darted over the raked earth in little forays here and there, worried and competent, brisking her tail. At the edge of the dead fire she sat up on her haunches. All of her trembled—paws and ears and the halo of her whiskers—not with fear, but with the intensity of being mouse.

Behind her every skirmish lay written in the dust by paw and tail. She had found nothing. Still she would search. Her eyes shone. As she groomed her belly Kat saw a double row of teats.

"Little mother," said Kat, hearing her own griev-ing voice, "what you need isn't here."

As though at a clapped hand the deer mouse jumped, spun, and dashed for the door. She wriggled under it.

Stiffly Kat rose and followed her. She tried the door.

It was unlocked. It had never needed to be locked. It opened soundlessly on the eastern sky, starry and lightening faintly along the shoulder of Dark Heart.

Kiku's snore was a small sound. The crickets were louder, singing to left, to right, behind Kat as she ran along the path. Her feet on the earth felt dreamy, weightless; yet she thought, looking behind her, that her footprints shone with cold light after she had passed.

I need my ivory seal, she thought. I want it back.

She was not hungry, but her legs felt loose at the hip. Across the stream, black as lichen, lay Creek, where at this moment the bear stirred in harness, Set stirred in sleep. The women were putting on their masks. In one window a lamp winked sud-denly orange. Kat ran faster, her skirt white, skin white, a moth.

Creek fell behind her across the water. She clambered over a stony outcrop and entered the juniper and oak, running like the deer mouse, thinking only, My seal, I want it.

The dawn wind was rising as she came to the Blessing Tree. The earth was a moil of shadows. Her bare feet were noiseless, and the water talked. Nothing looked like itself, and everything moved: prayer ribbons, shapeless bushes, fallen white branches. She ran past them around the huge tree to where the hill came down, wrinkled by roots. She found the beehive in the dark.

It had changed.

The bees had been building. Staring up through the paling air, Kat could not see where she had pressed the little seal. The fluted wattles and gills of wax had shifted like the banks of the creek after a flood. The hive was new.

She put up her hand. The black surface of the comb seethed with bees.

She withdrew her hand. She stood unmoving while everything around her moved—the wind in the underbrush, the roiling bees.

She thought, I'll knock that hive down! I'll get a stick!

In a shower of pebbles she slid to the poolside and snatched up a straight fallen branch.

Live as a snake it writhed from her, it jerked her forward. The night laid hands on her, grasping, groping; she screamed once, with her whole body, and wrenched away.

"Who is it?" a voice screamed back.

"Raim!"

His body in its black cloak took shape out of the crazy shadow, crouched half in the pool. His face and hands were wet. In the dull light they shone gaunt with longing.

"Kat—Demon ghost—"

"No."

"It's you! By the holy—she sent you!" The pale sky wheeled, not enough breath in it. He said, "You went to the bear?"

"No."

His face was triumphant, hard. "I knew you wouldn't. I knew you'd come to me. I prayed to be forgiven. Ouma sent you!"

"No!" It was the only word in her mouth.

"I won't profane her any more. She knows I need you. I've suffered. I can't, I can't live without you."

Silence.

"Kat!"

Her heel slipped a little on the gravel.

He turned his head, listening. In a sensible, flat voice he said, "I have to have you. It's owed me. I'm not cursed."

Her body sensed his leap before her mind did. He jumped; but when his blind grip fell she was gone, except for the hem of her skirt. She tore away, leaving him with his hands full of cloth.

"*Kat!*"

She slithered back under the bushes like the deer mouse, all reaction, no thought. He thrashed after her, but he was too big, too blind, the brush too thick. The rustle of her leaving was that of any small animal.

She crept backward. Through the bushes she could not see him throw down the torn skirt, but she heard him scream, in rage and pain, "*Do you think I'd live in the dark forever?*"

She heard him stumbling up the hunters' path, going quickly, as if it were not dark.

The stillness that flowed in after him spread and stood, solid as the mountain.

A bird woke, and sang one note. Fainting from its stars, the sky became what it was: empty air to fall through. Kat watched the ooze of blood from her cut hand slow, then darken, then cease.

She said, "Raím, no."

She tried to rise. She could not. The brush was too thick. She scrambled on all fours, upward through the thorns by the animal tracks.

He had too long a start. She would not take the hunters' path. She would make a shortcut across the Mother's lap and stop Raím before he reached the cliff.

She could not go straight. There were tree trunks, outcrops, boulders nubby with garnets and moss. Hawthorn, buckthorn, bloodthorn laced and interlocked. The trails meandered at a fox's whim; they seemed to lead her always to the right, up Dark Heart, so that she never came down as far as she went up. She did not know how far she had gone or where she was. The sky went white as milk, and the thorns went gray.

The thorns grew thick. They grew longer, and dragged along her back. She battered her way, bleeding—the track narrowing, the light rising, the east bright—until she could go no farther.

The way was shut. Thorns stabbed her arms. She backed up, stopped. The thorns seemed to close behind her. The least struggle drove barbs into her thighs. Half-crouched, she could not move.

"*Raím!*" she screamed.

There was no sound except the chuckle of a starling on a bough.

She let her body sink downward to be with her cold feet. There was nowhere else to go.

She thought, I chose this path. Maybe it's brought me to death, but at least it's mine, finally. The same for Raím. He made his choice. I can't save him.

She laid her head on her forearms, remembering the black tunnel in the Tells.

With her eyes on a level with the roots she could see another tunnel, not in earth but in thorns—a dark track barely wider than her face. It led upward.

Like a snake in a hole she twisted and followed it. Thorns clawed her, but as long as she did not rise from her belly she could move, not toward Raím but somewhere, unknown, up Dark Heart.

Each twig had a glittering edge. In the crest of the thicket the birds were shouting, rattling down the dew. Among the roots Kat went by the only way there was, on thighs and elbows streaked with blood.

The thorn ceiling lifted. She rose to a crawl. The path grew grassy, and it opened before her as a cleft. She crawled on as the way became a corridor, slightly expanding. At the end of it stood luminous aspen, green and gold, with white trunks and tender leaves, and a glimpse of meadowy light like a door.

In front of the door something moved, restless as a fly at a window latch.

She stopped in her tracks. So did that thing stop, whatever it was, black.

Gooseflesh pricked her back. Was it wolf? Wild dog? Was it the bear?

She looked to right and left. All thorns—no way out. She looked behind her at her trampled, impossible trail.

She thought, Even if I could go back, I'd just be stuck where I was before.

She half stood. The grass brushed her bloody knees as she walked forward, calling, "Brookie! Brookie!" in a voice from a dream.

For it looked like a cat. Then like a wolf. It looked like a bear, was not a bear, was a fist of blackness with a yellow eye, a red and open mouth. It had teeth. It drooled and gasped, seeing her; it paced between her and the meadow's green.

She walked toward it in terror that was past terror, knowing it was hers. It grew larger as she came nearer to it.

She stepped into the clearing among the gesturing trees and laid her hands on its black fur.

Its face was level with her own. Its clean stink panted over her. She pushed her fingers into the dense coat, touched the whiskers that were springy as a seal's, the wet snout. Four thick legs gripped the ground; she saw dark testicles, a double row of teats. Sexless and sexual, full of all the energy of the wild, it stood with each hair vivid, shining in the morning; she stroked back the fur from its foreign, living eyes.

"Oh, you beautiful," she said.

The beast yawned. It grew.

"Body like my body," said Kat. "Yes." As the mouth widened and the white teeth lengthened, she leaned into them as though into a cave that was not dead but living, full of breath and pain. The white teeth came down. There was agony, and darkness, and the trail of her footprints ended there.

20

STARS SWARMED in the branches like bees. Silver water rang into the pool, beginning its long wandering to the sea.

The old snake that holed among the roots of the big cottonwood slid homeward after a night's hunting. At the muddy place below the watercress it paused, tasting the wind with its tongue. Something lay across the path. The snake shifted course, slid around it, and poured down its hole. It did not hurry, for the thing lay so still: the body of a young woman with red hair—naked, scratched by brambles, curled up like a mouse.

Dark Heart rose behind her, ancient and new.

Like a dreaming dog Kat whined and woke herself. Her shoulder was in the mud, and the grass tickled her. The sun began, once more, to rise upon the Blessing Tree.

A jay in the juniper squalled, *"There! There!"* until its voice was Jekka's and feet came running and it *was* Jekka, with Bian.

"She took you herself. She found you and took you!" Sobbing, Bian lifted Kat's shoulders onto her lap. Behind her in the pale light the women of Creek huddled, silent. "You are our sister in Ouma now!"

Bian's words were a flock of birds in the wind; they tumbled and fluttered, settling slowly onto the branches of language. Gazing up at Bian, Kat said, "It wasn't a bear."

Bian trembled. "I will call it a bear! I will *make* it be a bear!"

The women of Creek made the sign against cursing.

Kat said, "It wasn't a demon, either."

But Bian's arms were rigid, beginning to withdraw.

"How can a child know good from evil? If it wasn't a demon, what was it?"

Slowly Kat sat up. The morning light was rising, soft on every twig and bud.

"It was being alive," she said. "It was me. I had paws, and I ran, I ran."

She remembered Dark Heart like a universe: the scent of mornings, of fern wallow and blood and stone. The wind had whispered and she had understood it. She had felt mud breathe; she had lapped silence like clear water. The mountain was a loom of countless threads, and she was part of it. Dark Heart was hers.

Then, as she had given herself to the beast, it gave itself to her. The being that was both of them had come down through the thickets to the Blessing Tree, and there it had surrendered its wild body to become just Kat, with dirty knees.

But it was like a dream, the images fading back. Kat said, "I don't want to forget it!"

"Paws?" said Bian. "If there were paws then it *was* a bear!"

Kat put her arms around her aunt's shoulders. "I think you can call it anything you like."

Bian covered her face. "How can I love you now? I don't know who you are!"

"Well, *I* know," said Kat. "Enough to be going on with." She stroked Bian's hair and saw gray in it. "I don't suppose there's any raspberry cake left?"

"Tcha!" said Bian.

The mountain clearing was wide with dawn, loud with birds. Kat felt light and simple; she was naked and did not mind it, clothed in her scars. "How long was I gone?" she said.

"Three days." Bian was weeping again. "We found blood, the smashed jar, your skirt all torn."

Kat said, "Raím."

"He's gone." The voice was Wenta's, hoarse and old. "We thought . . . I don't know what we thought. We didn't know whether to search for you, or curse, or pray. Then Set came to tell us that Raím's hearth was cold. We thought you had run away together. Where could you go, a girl and a blind man? But 'away' is enough destination, when you're young. Then this morning Jekka found you and brought us here. But Raím—" Wenta flinched. "They say he kept going back to the cliff where he . . . and I don't want to think . . ."

"That's where you'll find him," said Kat.

But she knew only where to find his body—what little would be left of the warm face she had kissed. Tears filled her eyes and spilled. She thought, Wherever his spirit is now, I hope it is flying.

"Call it a blessing," Wenta said. Her own eyes were wet. "We'll send the men to bring him home."

She looked around her at the other women. Then she held out to Kat her bony old hand. "Sister, can you stand?"

Kat took her hand and rose. The women of Creek came forward slowly and washed her in the pool at the foot of the Blessing Tree, singing the songs that made her safe for them.

The light grew colored and bright. Someone—it was Esangi—passed Kat a vest and kirtle. She put them on still warm; never her own clothes, always borrowed, but she did not mind that now.

They marked her breasts with honey and clay. She thought of the ivory seal, shrouded in sweetness, and said good-bye to it. She did not need a talisman anymore.

"Sister," said Wenta, "will you be tattooed?"

"I am tattooed."

Jekka stood at Kat's elbow, her once-merry face full of deference and fear.

"Jekka," said Kat, "don't look like that! It's only me."

Jekka shook her head. "Don't tell me where you've been. It's too peculiar." Bravely she added, "But you can still have my green glass necklace. If you want."

"Why did you look for me here?"

"I didn't. I came to pray that you'd be happy, whatever happened. And here you were. I thought you were dead. I ran! I've got such a stitch in my side." Jekka frowned. "And I thought I wanted a little sister! Stupid me."

"Come home," Bian said to Kat, and kissed her timidly. "We'll carry you."

"I can walk." All the grass was new. The water in the creek babbled among blackbirds and ducks; it wet Kat's feet. Word had gone ahead; on the far bank, under the Tells, the men were waiting. Emmot stepped forward.

Set stepped back. His face looked older, like Raím's face, raked by pain. The women began to sing the bringing-home song, as they caught the tang of wood smoke from the fires.

Kat stopped. Behind her the procession jumbled to a halt.

"Brook," said Kat.

There was uncertainty, consternation. "The brook? The creek?"

"The cat. I have to get Raím's cat."

"Set will go get it." But Set was backing away, shaking his head.

"No, I will." Kat turned and began to climb the hummocks of the Tells.

"Sister!" said Bian. "Come out of that place. You've been given back to us—will you leave us?"

"Let her go," said Wenta. "She knows what she needs."

Kat looked back. "I'll be home for breakfast," she said, and was gone over the first rise.

Among the stones the grass sprang green. Weeds whipped her legs, rabbits ran, a pheasant rose with a shout. The badger glowered from his den as she dipped into the little corrie and found the rosebush with its toothy new leaves. The old brown skull was upended, full of a deer-mouse nest. The babies squeaked.

"Thank you, sister," said Kat.

She picked up the grinding stone. Carrying it in the crook of her elbow, she came over the last hill and saw the bothy, cold-chimneyed, with a black and open door.

She stood under the hissing poplars. Raím's shirt had blown against the wall, and sand was beginning to cover it. Across the bucket his razor lay waiting for him. The rain barrel stood empty. His footprints tracked this way and that in the dried mud.

He was all around the place. Trembling, she called, "Brookie," with barely a breath. Wind made the door creak.

Green grass, morning,
I see you, I see.

She heard the ghostly tune. The hair rose on her neck, her back prickled, and her eyes went dark.

"*White sun, noonday,*" Raím's voice sang. Then it cried, "The devil! You meddling rag—give me that! Get out!" Brook shot from the door, furious, and veered up a polar trunk.

"Raím!"

Kat dropped the grinding stone. There was a

sound of blundering inside the house, a crash. She ran into the bothy. He was struggling to rise from the wreck of the stool that had tripped him. She lifted him in her arms.

Gaunt, unshaven, he said in a hoarse voice over and over, "I'm sorry, I had no right, I'm sorry. . . ."

She said over and over, "You were dead. I thought you were dead."

"I couldn't do it. I got to the edge and I couldn't *see*." He held her newly scarred hand in both his hands. It hurt her. "I don't know anything. I couldn't jump."

"I'm glad."

A little light came into his haggard face. "On the loom—as much yarn as I could untangle by myself—it's for you." She looked beyond him and saw a slender new warp, a plane of cloth barely started—just enough to show, brown on cream, the track of the deer mouse. With her hand to his lips he said, "Kat. I can't ask, not after what I did. I have to learn a new way to weave." He moved her hand to his heart. "On *this* loom. But—"

She said gently, "No."

"Set?"

"Not Set."

"The singer." He stooped over her hand, rigid. "You'll go back to him."

"Maybe. Not yet. I have to learn a little more."

"Learn a little more," he said, his face straining. She touched his face.

"Cry, Raím," she said, and he cried.

Turn the page for a sneak peek at the next book in

Listening at the Gate

By Betsy James

Smell of the nape
of your neck, of your hair,
rise and fall
of your side with the tide
of your breath,
warmth of you all up the front
of the warmth of me—
see,
see,
see in the dark,
see in the dark without eyes.

—Winter Dreaming Croon, the Rigi

"YOU CAME BACK," he said. "I knew you would. You have grown up, grown beautiful."

"You don't know that, it's dark, you can't see me—"

"Oh, I see you."

It was his hand he was seeing with, gentle as an eye. But I felt Queelic's hand, I heard Queelic scream *She's horrible!* as he wiped and wiped to get me off himself.

Nall's hand found the scars. Went still. I tried to push it away.

It would not be pushed. "What made these?"

I was ashamed as dirt. I said, "A bear."

He drew a hissing breath, moved his hand along the puckered lines.

"Don't!" But if I pulled away, I would fall into the sea. "I'm sorry—It's—In the place where I was, every girl has to be eaten by a bear—"

"Eaten," he said. "Some holy thing?"

"Yes! A ceremony. But it went wrong, it didn't happen the way it was supposed to—"

"Eaten, yet not eaten. As I was killed, yet not killed."

"Yes." I felt relief like rescue and, still, such shame. "But I'm so sorry—"

"To be scarred? Kat. Look." He made me look with my hand as he had, guiding it to the marks of rope on his wrists, the lines on back and thigh left by the rocks the surf had tumbled him through. He drew me down to feel his right foot; it was covered with a skein of ridges like a tangled net.

"It never healed right," he said. "I am lame."

Then I understood his lurching run.

He said, "Every holy passage leaves a scar."

The world got huge, and clean, and me clean in it. I put my hands on his feet and said, stammering, "Don't you dare let them scorn you! You're a *seal*. On land you're *supposed* to lollop along."

He laughed; he laughed till he sat down backward.

He kissed my scars. Around us the ocean burst and roared.

"Oh," I said, "wherever did you *come* from?"

"From the Gate!"

I heard the big letter. "What Gate?"

"My ama would smack you for asking," he said, and laughed more. He put his arms around me and drew me up to stand leaning against the warmth of him.

I did not believe any of this, not even the sea itself. I began to laugh too—or maybe cry. "Ama? What's an ama?"

"A great-grandmother. Mine. Smaller even than you, with white hair and a hard hand. And the Gate is the truth of the world, you Leagueman's child!"

"Tell me the truth of the world," I said. If anybody knew it, he would. Anything he said would be truth.

He put his lips to my ear, I could hear him smiling. "Are you listening?"

I was.

"The Gate is two stones in the sea. It lies west of the last island of all, at the world's edge. Two stones in the sea—and everything that is, is born from it: seals, and cows, and Leaguemen, and songs. The whole world. You." He touched his mouth to mine. "And me. From the Gate I came. I wanted to. My mother and father made my body, and my ama smacked me and told me not to meddle, and I meddled, and the Reirig with his elders killed me, and you called me, and I came, and you kissed me, and now you have come back to me, and I shall kiss you, kiss you."

This he did. I could hardly stand, crazy with him, shaking.

"And now you have been reborn from a bear—"

"Eaten! Eaten and given back—"

"Spit back out, I think. It was your red hair. That bear's mouth burned! It spat you—"

"Ptah!"

"Bear Spit. Is that what your name is now?"

I hit him with my soft fist. But he was stronger, he could trap both my hands in one of his and tickle until I squealed and then sobbed in earnest, because Ab Harlan was a nightmare and Nall was real.

He held me. Then he wiped my eyes with his knuckles, kissed me again, and said, "Let's go, Bear Spit. Dai is waiting."

"Dai—oh—Dai—"

"He was behind Eb the brewer, on the horse that passed us. Didn't you hear him laugh? The bull was chasing that blond boy." Nall laughed too and wiped his own eyes. "You've come home to the hornets' house!"

Sometimes he spoke fast and slangy, like a Downshoreman; sometimes quaintly, like a Rig. His hands smelled of tar, he was as full of life as a nut is of meat, and when I touched him, I thought my heart would stop. "Get into the *manat*, Bear Spit," he said.

"Manat?"

He turned to the little boat and slapped the hull. "Greased sealskin, from seals washed up dead on the beach—when there were still seals. Whalebone frame."

The round-bellied manat reminded me of Nondany's dindarion. "You made it?"

"I work at the shipyard. We build big, timid boats that hate to leave the shore, but for myself I built this." He lifted the manat into shin-deep water, pulled out the double-bladed paddle, and slid into the rear hatch as if he were pulling on trousers. "When I'm alone, I use two water skins to balance my weight. But with you in front it will trim just right."

He had built it knowing I would come back. I said, "Is there a paddle for me?"

He jumped out again and kissed me. "Take off your shoes."

I shed my wet sandals, waded into the sea, and stowed them in the stern. The little boat dipped and nodded. He steadied it against his thigh and showed me where to set my hands on the coaming of the front hatch.

I put one foot into the hull. It slid out from under me, dumping me on one knee in the baby waves.

He caught it as if it were a runaway pig. "Stay low. Keep your weight on your hands."

I tried again. The manat rocked wildly, as though it had no weight, and I did not dare step onto my foot.

Again he steadied the hull. "There is only one thing to know. The manat is *you*. A little skin and bone to keep the sea out—but you are its weight, its balance. You and I."

The boat bobbed, light as a cup. I took hold of the coaming again and thought myself in. The inside of the hull kissed one bare heel, then the other, and I sat down sweetly like a coot on the water.

"I knew it!" He tossed his paddle in the air, caught it, and gave it to me still warm from his hands. He began to push the manat away from the sandspit.

"Wait—aren't you coming?" I tried to jump up. The manat rolled over like a barrel.

He fished me out, spitting, and caught the escaping boat with the other hand. "I was coming. Now you can learn how to shake the water out."

I shivered, soaking wet, thinking how I had put out my hand to catch myself and felt it go through water as if through nothing. "If we tip over, we'll drown."

"We might."

Between us we dumped the water out of the manat, repacked it, and set it again on the sea. Paddle in hand, I held the coaming and hopped into the front hatch.

"Bear Spit," said Nall, and I knew it was praise. The boat's balance shifted as he entered it, steadying around our two bodies. At the corner of my eye I caught the flick of his paddle.

"You can use the blade to stop yourself from rolling over," said his voice behind me. "Shall I teach you? Or shall I be boatman for us both?"

"I want to be my own boatman. Boatwoman."

He showed me how to paddle myself back upright with my wooden fin. I could not do it, but it gave the water substance, something to push against. I thought of where I had been not long before, standing by a little creek that hurried to this sea.

"Home," said Nall. "Mailin's."

We pushed away from the sandy refuge. As my arms began to understand the stroke, I looked past the surfy skerries to the whole ocean, broad and black. The prow wavered like a compass needle around some point in the west, as though I had a destination, still formless, out there.

Author's Note

I began the stories that eventually became
The Seeker Chronicles when I was a teenager,
and hid them under the bed in a locked tin box.
Eventually I tore them up. But I did not forget them,
and years later, as a professional artist, I retold
them in a long series of narrative watercolors.
It is upon those stories and paintings
that these books are based.